Your Turn, Mr. Moto

BY JOHN P. MARQUAND

The Moto Series

YOUR TURN, MR. MOTO
THANK YOU, MR. MOTO
THINK FAST, MR. MOTO
MR. MOTO IS SO SORRY
LAST LAUGH, MR. MOTO
RIGHT YOU ARE, MR. MOTO

Selected Novels

THE LATE GEORGE APLEY
SINCERELY, WILLIS WAYDE

Your Turn, Mr. Moto

JOHN P. MARQUAND

LITTLE, BROWN AND COMPANY
BOSTON   TORONTO

REPUBLISHED JULY 1985

Library of Congress Cataloging in Publication Data

Marquand, John P. (John Phillips), 1893–1960.
    Your Turn, Mr. Moto.

    I. Title.
PS3525.A6695Y6 1985   813'.52   85-86
ISBN 0-316-54697-6

BP

*Published simultaneously in Canada
by Little, Brown & Company (Canada) Limited*

PRINTED IN THE UNITED STATES OF AMERICA

Your Turn, Mr. Moto

CHAPTER I

COMMANDER JAMES DRISCOLL, attached to the Intelligence branch of the United States Navy, has asked me to write this, in order that my version may be placed in the files with his own account of certain peculiar transactions which took place in Japan and China some months ago. My immediate reaction, when Driscoll made the request, is the same as it is now. I had a vision of certain executives in the service reading this sort of thing. I told Driscoll that no one would believe it, and his answer, if not a compliment to me, was partially reassuring.

"Maybe," he said, "but I have a hunch they will. You'll probably write it so badly that they'll know it is the truth."

"But it's preposterous," I said. "It's melodrama. Honest to goodness — no one in his right mind, Driscoll, if he isn't in the scenario department of

3

some movie outfit, writes this sort of stuff."

Driscoll thought a moment. The idea appeared to interest him so much that I believe he has really thought of writing fiction in his softer moods.

"Don't let that worry you," he said finally. "It wouldn't go. Any sort of narrative has to have a hero in it to get over with the public, and, believe me, you weren't any hero. Oh, no, you don't need to be self-conscious for once in your life. Just snap into it. It won't take you long. Besides, there's another angle to this sort of thing. Probably no one will ever read it, anyway."

"Then why do I write it?" I inquired. Curiously enough, this question seemed ridiculous to Driscoll. He reminded me that I had been in the service myself at the time of the World War and that I should understand about army and navy paper work.

"You can just go right ahead," he said comfortably, "with the almost complete assurance that the whole thing will be stored away somewhere in a room in Washington. Why, if I can possibly avoid it, I won't read it myself."

"Thanks," I said, "but how do I begin?"

His answer, though practical, has proved of no great help.

"You sit down with a pen and ink and paper, and you write it. You can still form your letters, can't you? You tell what happened, Lee."

So that's what I am doing. I'm using Driscoll's time-worn phrase of snapping into it. I am trying to cast back into this series of incidents which occurred on the other side of the Pacific Ocean, but although the pieces have all been fitted quite completely together, when I try to start, the elements of this artificial beginning are as mysterious as the beginning was in fact. My mind lingers on certain incidents. I think of a suave scion of the Japanese nobility named Mr. Moto, if that is his real name. I think of a dead man in the cabin of a ship; the roaring of a plane's motor comes drumming across my memory, and I hear voices speaking in Oriental tongues. The past of an ancient race mixes peculiarly with the present. And in back of it all I see a girl, — one of those amazing wanderers in our modern world, disinherited and alone. International espionage moves in a world of its own, and its characters must always be lonely.

5

"Under-cover work is always like that," Driscoll said to me once. "The people one encounters are much the same. They may be shady and raffish, but don't forget they're all of them brave. They do their work like pieces on a chess-board and nothing stops them from moving along their diagonals. You mustn't feel animosity toward them, Lee, for they feel none toward you. They're working for their respective countries and that's more than a lot of people do."

Perhaps what is still the most interesting part of this adventure is its complete impersonality, its lack of rancor. I believe honestly that if Mr. Moto, a most accomplished gentleman, and I were to meet today that we might enjoy each other's company; and I should be glad to drink with him in one of his minute wine cups to the future of Japan. I have an idea that he would agree with me heartily in wishing for perpetual amity between Japan and the United States, as long as that amity did not interfere with what he and his own political faction conceive to be his nation's divine mission to establish a hegemony in the East. Distance sometimes makes it difficult to remember that Japan is a very great

6

country and that the Japanese are capable people, sensitive and intelligent. Still, although it sometimes seems incredible that our two nations should ever go to war, there is always the thought of war behind the scenes in every nation. Given a shift in the balance of power, men like Moto must start working, I suppose.

But I am getting away from my beginning.

Probably I had better start in the Imperial Hotel at Tokio one afternoon in spring about a year ago. Out of some confused notes which I made at the time I have been able to rescue the essential dates and scenes. With their help and my memory, I'll do the best I can.

In the first place, I suppose I must tell who I am and what I was doing in Tokio one spring afternoon. Though time moves fast and characters appear and disappear in a hasty procession before the public eye, the readers of the newspapers for the past decade may be vaguely familiar with my name. I am the "Casey" Lee whom various publicity directors have touted as a war ace. My first name incidentally is not "Casey" but Kenneth C. Lee — K.C.

—not that it makes much difference. I am the Casey Lee who flew the Atlantic at a time when previous flyers had rather taken the first bloom off that feat. My reputation and my personality used to be as carefully built up in those days as a pugilist's or a motion-picture star's, for my personality meant money. In short, I was one of that rather unfortunate group of almost professional heroes who sprang up in the boom days after the war and whose exploits diverted a jaded and somewhat disillusioned nation. I was a stunt flyer, having been a Chasse pilot in the war, a transcontinental flyer and a transatlantic flyer with a row of American and Italian war medals besides. My picture looked well in the rotogravure sections. My testimonial looked well in the advertisements of clothing and lubricants and nourishing foods, but when the cloud of depression grew blacker, people quite reasonably seemed to grow tired of heroes. I was pushed more and more into the background with others of my kind. Thus, it was not strange that when money was running very short and a large tobacco company offered me the chance of making a flight from Japan to the United States, I should have welcomed the opportunity. I welcomed it even though I had no great conviction that I was any longer in a suitable condition to go through with such a business. I was only glad to attempt it because I was rather tired of life. That was why I was in Tokio, in a country which was entirely strange to me, waiting for a plane to be shipped from the States and for the usual publicity to start.

I can still see the yellow stonework and the curious floor levels and galleries in the Imperial Hotel and their strange sculptured decorations, half modernistic and half Oriental. I can see the intelligent, concentrated faces of the waiter boys and the outlandish mixture of guests, — Europeans from the embassies, tourists from a cruise ship, Japanese in European clothes, Japanese girls in flowered kimonas, Japanese men in their native *hakimas*. That background of costume is startling when one stops to think of it. It is like the East and West meeting in two waves of unrelated cultures which swirl about Tokio's streets.

It was a fine sunny day outside, I can remember. It occurred to me that I had been drinking heavily since early in the morning, but this state was not unusual with me. At the time of the war we pilots had

9

drunk in the evening to forget the imminence of death, and after that most of us had continued, to forget the imminence of boredom. I think we had a reasonable semblance of an excuse. When one starts air fighting at the age of eighteen the values of life are apt to become distorted. One craves for the thrill of excitement as the nerves of an addict clamor for his favorite drug. I cannot feel so badly about the drinking of those days.

It was the drinking that I had done to drown the depression that inevitably follows a man unlucky enough to become a publicized hero of which I cannot boast. Liquor had become a problem to me, when, after weeks and months of every sort of adulation for having made a transatlantic flight, I was dropped as suddenly as if a wing had come off my plane. The depression which follows the excitement is the worst of it. In those moments of letdown I could sometimes see myself as I must have appeared to others, — not Casey Lee, one-time war ace, who had fought in Poland and Spain against the Riffs, nor Lee the ocean pilot, but only a shell of that Casey Lee.

I remember that I was talking. There was a crowd

around me as usual, of people who had nothing better to do than listen to me talk, and who enjoyed the association with a celebrity even if he might have been a trifle seedy.

"The plane's being shipped next week, a new type Willis Jones AB-3," I was telling them. "Give me another week to tune her up and I'm ready for it. I'll take her across alone, straight on the shipping lane, with one stop at Honolulu. The Pacific isn't any worse than the Atlantic, if you fly high, I guess."

"Will you have another drink, Mr. Lee?" someone said.

"Yes," I answered, "I will have another drink. I'm perfectly glad to have several more. Does anybody here think I can't fly the Pacific?"

"Oh, no, Mr. Lee," came a voice from the crowd; "of course not."

"There's only one thing that can stop me," I said, "and that's money, and I've got the financial backing this time. Give me a crate to fly and refueling planes and I'll fly a non-stop around the world."

"Why not make it twice around the world, Mr. Lee?" another voice said.

With a little difficulty I focused my attention on

the speaker. He was a pale pimply youth whom I had never seen before, obviously an American. "Listen, baby," I said to him. "You're the only product that America's turned out since 1918. When I see you, I know the United States is going to hell. I don't have to listen to your lip. Everybody knows who I am."

"Of course they do, Mr. Lee," said someone. "Won't you have another drink?"

"Yes," I said, "I don't mind if I do. Always glad to have another drink, always glad to try anything once or twice — that's me."

"Tell us," said someone respectfully, "who is backing you this time?"

"It's a cigarette company," I said. "They're using a part of their advertising appropriation for a transpacific flight. Believe me, it's the first break I've had in a long time. The mayor of Tokio gives me a couple of packages of their cigarettes, or somebody in Tokio, I don't remember who. And I deliver one pack to the Governor of Hawaii and another to the Mayor of New York City. I'm going to be a goodwill ambassador between Japan and the United States. But I don't care so long as I have a crate to fly. The good old American game of nonsense doesn't bother me."

"You needn't yell about it so," a voice objected. "You're an American, aren't you?"

"That is where I was born," I answered, "but I'm broadminded enough to have my own ideas. I've fought for the Spaniards and the Poles. There are other nations besides the United States — in case you don't know — several others."

"All right, Lee," said someone, "but here you are in a public place. Keep your voice down. A lot of these Japanese are looking at you."

"Let 'em look," I said. "Why should I care if they look? And I'll say anything I damn well please any time at all."

As I spoke, I became aware that my voice must have been louder than I had intended. I saw individuals staring at me curiously and I set down my glass. I was reaching a stage, which I had known before, when I became sorry for myself. And I had a sufficiently good reason to be sorry for myself half a minute later. One of the hotel boys, bowing and drawing in his breath noisily between his teeth, presented me with a cable. The words were slightly blurred and I had to concentrate to make them clear, before I could understand their meaning. The cable was signed by the codeword of the cigarette company. "Plans for flight off," it said. "Bank will pay your passage home."

My first thought was one of sickening hopelessness, for I had not realized until I saw that cablegram how much I had counted on this opportunity. It had raised me in my own estimation above other flying men I knew, and it offered me a prospect of redeeming myself in the eyes of others. I knew well enough why I had been selected,—on account of my name and my past reputation, not because of any present ability or future promise. I even had a sufficiently uncomplimentary idea of myself to suspect why the plan had been vetoed. I could hear them in New York saying that Casey was through. It seemed to me that everything was over then; I could see myself returning to the rôle I had played for several years, living on an outworn reputation. I suppose whoever we are, we try to rationalize all our failures. We push away our own faults and try to blame them on someone else. That is exactly what I did then. In some irrational way, I attributed my own failure directly to my country and to my country's eccentricities. The group around my table was looking at me curiously as I stared up from that cable. I tried to return casually to the subject where we had left off, a difficult matter when the words of that cable were ringing, with the drinks I had taken, through my thoughts.

"Since when was it a sin to criticize one's country?" I inquired. "I'm tired of having everyone wince and look scared, if a word is said in public against the present Administration. If it represents the will of America, it is not the country that I used to know. The United States are in the hands of a lot of communized visionaries, if you want my idea. I'm not afraid to say I'm ashamed of certain aspects of my country. I could tell you a thing or two about what's happened to commercial aviation. Can you sit here and admit that my country has not repudiated its just obligations to its citizens by juggling with its currency? The word of the United States isn't what it used to be, and the sooner we all know it the better. The national character isn't what it used to be, and I can prove it by this cable in my hand. Now that our government can repudiate its obligations, any citizen seems to feel free to break an agreement any time — as long as the man he breaks it with can't get back at him."

"What's the trouble, Lee?" someone asked. Even in my stimulated state, I felt that I had become involved beyond my depth, and that I had made a statement which I could not back by intelligent argument. I was no expert on the problems of currency and I realized that the economic woes of the world were as insoluble as my own.

"Those double-crossers back home," I said. "They've turned me down."

"Maybe they heard something," a voice suggested. "You've been raising a good deal of hell, Lee."

There was no doubt that the remark was true, but its implication was enough to make me lose my temper in a way I never had done before. I could see myself going straight down the ladder without friends and without respect. I whirled upon the man who spoke and I shouted at him. In my total lack of self-control I did not care for consequences. I did not care where I was or who heard me.

"Some damn sneak like you has been telling stories on me!" I shouted. "By God, do Americans have to have Boy Scout masters and Sunday-school teachers to fly for them? To hell with you! To hell with the whole bunch of you! And particularly my fellow citizens."

I could see that my last remark shocked them, and now I can understand why. National solidarity becomes important in direct ratio to the distance we are away from home.

"Be quiet, Lee!" one of the group said.

"Who for? You?" I answered.

"No, for yourself. You shouldn't slam your country in a foreign place."

"And who's going to stop me?" I shouted back.

That was when I saw an American naval officer had joined us, a former friend of mine. He must have heard me talking. I had not seen Jim Driscoll for years, but we had served together in the war as naval aviators on the Italian front. I knew him right away when he walked up to my table, — a trim stocky man in a white uniform, with commander's stripes and a heavy determined face. "So you're drunk again, are you, Casey Lee?" Jim Driscoll said.

As I say, I remembered Driscoll well enough. To

see him appear just then out of nowhere was like a final blow by destiny to my own self-esteem. We had started even once. I had been a better man than Driscoll back in the war, and now we stood there, both changed by the pitiless marks of time, — Driscoll a commander in the navy, and myself an arrant failure.

"Not too drunk to know you, Jim," I answered.

Jim Driscoll had put on weight since I had seen him last, and was too heavy for flying now. He had assumed an expression that I had seen others of my own friends wear of late. In it there was a hint of pity, and it annoyed me that Driscoll should pity me or should be in a position to administer reproof.

"Casey," Jim Driscoll said, "I used to think you were the bravest man in the world. You'd better sleep it off. You wore the uniform once."

"The luckiest thing I ever did was to get out of it," I told him. "It gives me a chance to say what I think. It's more than you can do, Driscoll, and you can remember that I'm not one of your enlisted men. You heard me; what are you going to do about it? I don't like my country."

"I can tell you what I think of you," Driscoll

18

answered. "You're making yourself into a public disgrace as well as nuisance. If I weren't leaving for Shanghai tonight, I'd see if your passport couldn't be revoked."

I took my passport out of my pocket, tore it straight across and tossed it on the floor.

"And that's what I care for my passport," I said. "There are plenty of other countries. Take Japan — Japan's a nice country."

But Jim Driscoll paid no more attention to me. He had turned a stiff back and was walking steadily away. Then I saw that I was alone at the table where I had been sitting, deserted by everyone I knew.

It dawned on me that I had gone much further than I had intended, beyond the bounds of reason or decorum, in my criticism. I had spoken in a maudlin way, when I would much better have kept my ill-regulated thoughts to myself. Now that the damage had been done, I was too proud to retract a single word, if my life had depended on it. If they wanted to judge me by what I said in my cups, I would let them judge me.

Two Japanese army officers were staring at me

fixedly. Also a short dark man with his hair cut after the Prussian fashion — a habit which so many Japanese have adopted — was seated at a table near me, regarding me with curiosity. He was dressed in a cutaway coat and wore tiny patent-leather shoes. There was a signet ring on his left hand. I saw him look down at this ring and back at me again. I remember thinking that he seemed like a Japanese trying to masquerade as a continental European and not succeeding very well. He raised his hand as I watched and beckoned to one of the clerks behind the desk. The clerk hurried to him and bowed. Then the clerk turned to me.

"Perhaps you are tired, Mr. Lee?" the clerk said. "Will you have someone conduct you to your room?"

Then I found myself being helped to my room, whether I liked it or not, by the clerk and the small man in the frock coat, one on each side of me.

"It is too bad," the small man said. "I am very, very sorry."

I did not know until later that it was Mr. Moto who was speaking to me. I still do not know his exact rank, but he was a gentleman, no matter what his race might be.

"I am sorry," said Mr. Moto again, "very, very sorry. You will be better after a little sleep, perhaps."

He spoke sharply to the hotel clerk and the man bowed in a way that made me realize even in my condition that Mr. Moto was a man of importance.

"You may go now," he said to the clerk, "and understand, this gentleman is to have anything he may want."

The door closed softly behind him and I found myself sitting on the edge of the bed, with little Mr. Moto standing attentively before me. I have never felt so much an alien, for the conviction was growing upon me that I was cut off from everything I had ever known before. I, a man without a country, was closed into one of the curiously furnished rooms of the Imperial Hotel with that Japanese who exactly fitted into the surroundings.

I looked up to find him still gazing at me thoughtfully. I wondered what he wanted. I wished, with a sudden intensity, that he would go away.

The furniture was of some light-colored unvarnished hard wood. There was a built-in dresser, showing an odd unsymmetrical arrangement of cubbyholes for clothing. There were several chairs with legs short enough to accommodate a low-statured race. A writing table was covered with hotel notices in both English and Japanese. Beside the bed was a pair of hotel slippers, reminding me that the Japanese spent a large portion of their life in changing from one set of footwear to another. I looked at the man again. I still wished he would go away.

"May I help you to bed, perhaps?" he asked.

"No," I answered. "What's your name?"

He smiled deprecatingly. "Moto," he replied. "That is my name, please, and I should be glad to assist you. I was once a valet to several American gentlemen in New York." He knelt down and began to unlace my shoes. "Please," he said, "thank you. America is a magnificent country."

"Maybe," I said. "But it's thrown me over flat, Mr. What's-your-name."

"Moto," he repeated patiently.

"Well," I said, "you're not a valet here in Japan."

"No," said Mr. Moto, "but Americans always interest me. I saw that you were not well and that your friends had left you."

"Listen, Mr. Moto," I said, "when they can't get

anything more out of you, Americans always go away."

"It was not kind of them," Mr. Moto said. "I am sorry."

"Mr. Moto," I told him, "suppose you stop saying you're sorry. What do you want with me?"

"Only to assist you," he explained. "You are a foreigner, a guest, in my country, who has met with misfortune. Everyone knows who you are, of course. We have a great respect for American aviators." He drew in his breath with a peculiar little hiss. Even though he was dressed as a European and acted like one, he could not avoid some of the involuntary courtesies of his race. "I have seen you before. I think last night, in fact. I saw you dancing with a girl — a very beautiful girl with yellow hair. Was she not a Russian?"

I cast back into my mind with difficulty, trying to remember the hazy events of the night before. For a longer while than I cared to remember days and nights were hazy. They were made up of afternoons of drinking at some bar, cocktails before dinner somewhere, and more drinks, and then oblivion. Then I remembered that there had been a girl, a nice girl. My embarrassment, as I recalled what had happened, made me speak of her casually, as though she belonged to a lower class, but I knew better, nevertheless.

"Yellow hair?" I said. "Oh, yes, I met her somewhere. Yes, her name was Sonya. I don't know her last name — one of those Russian names. We got on very well until — well, I wasn't myself last night. She tossed me over when I made a pass at her. All right — what do I care? She might have known I didn't mean anything by it. Everybody's tossed me over!"

"Please," Mr. Moto said, inhaling through his teeth, "here are your pajamas. . . . You made a pass at her — I do not understand the phrase. Will you explain it, please?"

"Haven't you ever made a pass at anyone?" I inquired. "You might have, Mr. Moto. Since you're so curious, I don't mind telling you that I tried to kiss her in a taxicab. That's making a pass. She made the driver stop and got out and left me flat. I'm sorry about it, if you care to know."

"How do you mean?" said Mr. Moto. "She left you flat?"

"The way you see me now, Moto," I said. "I'm much obliged to you, but I wish you'd go. I want to go to sleep. I want to forget I was ever born."

I must have been half asleep then, but it seemed to me I could remember Mr. Moto moving carefully about my room. I was in a stupor, I suppose, somewhere between sleep and waking, with the fumes of Japanese-made whisky curling like mist through my consciousness. I seemed to be in an airdrome, in the cockpit of a fighting plane, ready to take off over the Austrian lines. Then, for no good reason, I seemed to be sitting on the lowered top of an automobile, riding along Broadway with the air full of ticker tape and torn-up telephone directories. I could hear the crowd shouting and a man in a cutaway coat like Mr. Moto's was making a speech. "America is very proud of you, Casey Lee," he was saying. Plenty of people were proud of me in those days. They were proud to have me at Newport and Southampton. They were proud to have me examine new tri-motor planes. They were proud to have me autograph books. It only came to me later that they were proud to take my money. I wondered what had happened to those days. They

25

had moved away from me into a series of speak-easies and club barrooms, leaving me finally — there was no use mincing matters — a broken-down adventurer. For no reason, I suppose, except because Mr. Moto's question had made me remember her, I thought of that girl of the other night. She had been the best-looking girl in the room, and the best-looking girl had never been any too good for me. And who was this girl? A Russian *émigrée,* a spy perhaps; Japan was full of spies. At some time while these thoughts raced, I must have gone to sleep. Sleep was the closest thing to being dead, and I wished that I were dead.

CHAPTER II

I WAS AWAKENED at 12.30 the next afternoon. I remember the time because I looked at my wrist watch. Someone was knocking on my door and the sound waked me. My door must have been unlocked, because one of the hotel boys was standing beside my bed when I opened my eyes. I had all the usual physical feelings of having been drunk the night before. My head was aching and my hands were shaking.

"If you please, sir," the boy was crying.

I pointed a quivering finger toward my bureau, and observed, to my surprise, that my room was in perfect order, my clothes neatly folded instead of being strewn, as they customarily were, in every direction. Then I remembered Mr. Moto, who said he had been a valet in America.

"Wait a minute, boy," I said. "Do you see that flask on the bureau?" It was an old leather-covered

27

flask which I had carried ever since the war. "Pour me out a half tumbler of that quick!"

"Please, sir —" said the boy again.

"Do what I tell you!" I interrupted him. My nerves were jangling like discordant bells. "Pour it out and hand it here! Never mind a tumbler. Take the cup off the bottom and fill it up!"

I had to take the little cup in both hands when he handed it to me, but once the liquor was inside me it steadied me. My head cleared, my hands quieted, my muscles were again in some sort of coordination. Then I recalled the last afternoon, and that my backers had left me flat. For a moment I had the impossible hope that they had reconsidered, that the boy was bringing me a cable, but his next words removed such illusions.

"A lady is waiting for you, please," the boy said. "She sent you this, please." And he handed me a note.

I tore open the envelope and read it. I remember the writing still, — large, bold, and foreign.

"Where are you? Don't you remember you asked me for lunch? I am waiting. I am not used to be kept waiting. If you ever want to see me again, you had better hurry."

It was signed "Sonya." I had not the slightest recollection of having asked her or anyone else to lunch, but I had enough pride not to wish her to think I had forgotten.

"Run me a cold bath," I said, "and tell the lady I'll be out directly."

The cold bath did me good. When I stepped out of it, I felt better and younger, for the cold water seemed to have washed out some of the lines around my eyes. In fact, I was surprised how well I looked, considering the life I had been leading. There were signs of that life in my face, but my body had resisted most of it, and my muscles were still hard. I looked at the scar on my left shoulder where an Austrian machine-gun bullet had shattered my collarbone, and at the long gash in my right calf which had been torn by a splinter when I had crashed behind the lines, — but that was long ago.

A girl was waiting for me outside — a pretty girl — which made me remember that I must still possess some attraction. I dressed carefully in a blue serge suit. I said to myself, "After all, Casey Lee, you're still a man," and I walked out into the lobby, cheerfully, because I knew that soon I could have another drink. I even recall humming that song we used to sing in the evenings when flying men gathered.

"I'm Going to a Happy Land Where Everything is Bright, Where the Hangouts Grow on Bushes and We Stay Out Every Night."

The yellow stone had been transformed overnight, evidently for the arrival of some important guest. The pillars were decorated with artificial peach blossoms and crossed banners, — one the rising sun of Nippon and the other a flag which I did not know. There was a bustle of preparation in the lobby, engineered by khaki-clad army officers with boots and sabers, and men in cutaway coats holding silk hats, evidently from the government offices. All of them wore the same intent, worried expression which I had observed often among the Japanese, as though they were conscientiously determined that everything should be done with absolute correctness in the face of a critical world audience.

I did not notice the excitement much, however, but looked instead for the girl whom I had forgotten that I had asked to lunch. As I sought her out among the Japanese and foreigners sitting at the little tables, I discovered I did not remember what she looked like very well. I could only remember that she was really beautiful and that she had yellow hair. I moved at once toward the only girl I could see who answered that description and I knew she was the one because she was looking at me. She was a tall girl, almost lanky. Her hair was reddish gold. Her eyes, dark blue, gave the combined impression of being both shrewd and seductive. Her lips were painted a deep red, and her hands were very long and slender. She was dressed in a white tailored suit. Although there was nothing specific in her appearance to betray it, I knew she was not American. She had the social poise and the adamantine quality of a more sophisticated world. I knew that girl had been about and had seen strange sights — many of them not pleasant — and that she could take care of herself, probably, in any situation. I knew that she was a Russian, because I had seen her type often enough during my short stay in the Orient. I had seen her sort at fine dinners and in cheap dance halls but there was a similarity to all nationals of her sort. They were all aloof, but all charming companions, able to be agreeable in any mood, able to give one an adventurous sense of competence, and displaying at the same time their own sadness, for they were sad people who wandered without a country. I took her hand and bent over it, clicking my heels together, a trick I'd learned in Rome, and she smiled at me.

"You are late," she said. Except for a throaty catch in her voice, her English was perfect, and I imagine she would have done as well in half a dozen other languages. "Did you not remember you asked me for lunch?" She was looking half reproachful, half amused, but she patted the chair beside her and I sat down.

"Will you forgive me if I tell you something?" I asked her. "I was under the impression, the only time we met, that you did not like me."

"But you would not care if I liked you or not?" she inquired. "Would you, Mr. Lee?"

I looked at her thoughtfully and told the truth. "I'm not sure," I said. "Mademoiselle — ?" I stopped, because I could not remember her name.

"Have you forgotten my name already?" she

asked. "Karaloff. But you called me Sonya the other night."

"Perhaps," I suggested, "it will be just as well if we forget the other night. Where would you care to go to lunch? And will you have a cocktail, Mademoiselle?"

She smiled, white teeth, crimson lips, slightly slanting eyes. "Sonya," she said.

"You are very kind to me," I answered, " — Sonya."

"Perhaps," she said, "I wonder . . . I like you, Mr. Lee. I like brave men."

It seemed to me that there was a tinge of sarcasm in that last remark. The boy came, and she gave her order for a glass of sherry and I ordered a double Scotch. "Sonya," I suggested, "suppose we leave out the brave stuff. I'd rather be a coward today, and I'm afraid of you, if you want the truth."

She laughed softly and leaned toward me, so near that I could catch the scent of gardenia in her hair. "Why," she asked, "are you afraid?"

"Just a peculiar intuition," I said, and I meant it. "I shouldn't like to be in love with you."

She laughed again. She had that way of making

one seem scintillating even when one said nothing amusing. "You're a funny man," she said. "Why?"

I finished my drink and watched her before I answered. It seemed to me that I had never seen such a mobile face as hers, and I suspected its mobility. First, she had been watchful and her eyes had been hard and shrewd. Now she seemed to have tossed away that watchfulness. "Because you'd make a fool out of me," I said bluntly. "It's been done before."

"Perhaps," she said. She smiled at me and I could see gold lights dance behind the blue of her eyes. "Brave men are so apt to be children."

I cannot describe the way I felt. I seemed to be lost in the personality of that Russian girl, in spite of common sense and instinctive caution. "That doesn't flatter me," I said. "You probably come from a sophisticated world where people live on logic. You can't help being beautiful, can you?"

"Do you think I do?" she asked me — "Casey?"

"Yes," I said. "I wonder who you are, and I know that you won't tell me."

Her eyes grew hard for a moment and again she had that look of someone who could go through anything untouched. She seemed about to make an indiscreet remark and then checked herself.

"Perhaps I'm not what you think I am, altogether," she said. "Are you what I think you are, I wonder?"

"Does it make any difference?" I asked her. It amused me to observe how deliberately she brought the curve of the conversation back to me.

"Your country's done a great deal for you," she said. "You must love it very much."

I rose to her suggestion almost without thinking. "My country took me when I was a kid of eighteen," I said. "I wasn't a bad kid, either, Sonya. It jammed me into naval aviation and put me in a plane that wasn't fit to fly. They killed a lot of my friends, those planes that shouldn't have left the ground at flying school. Then my country sent me to the Italian Front, and when it unsettled me for any sort of useful living, it closed the door of the navy to me because I was just a kid without real officer's training. And now it's left me flat in Tokio; that's all my country's done for me. I'd give up my nationality any time."

She opened her handbag and drew out one of those

35

long Russian cigarettes. "You're joking, aren't you?" she asked.

"No," I said, "I was never more serious in my life."

When I leaned forward to light her cigarette, she bent over the match and rested her fingers on mine, it seemed to me longer than was necessary, but I did not mind the touch of her fingers. "A man without a country," she said. Her voice was genuine and sad. "I'm sorry."

"Well," I said, "I can take what's coming to me."

"Casey," she asked, "do you like Japan?"

"Yes," I said. "Japan's a country that deals with facts sensibly. By the way —" My attention was caught again by the artificial peach blooms and the flags in the lobby. "What's all the excitement here today?"

"Don't you read the papers?" She laughed. "It's the delegation from Manchukuo come to call on the Emperor. Do you feel as the American State Department does about Japan's adventure in Manchukuo?" That husky voice of hers was softly, playfully caressing, but her eyes were not.

"No," I answered promptly, and I meant it. "If

you knew my country better, you would understand that it's characteristic of it to take a holier-than-thou-attitude. Before 1906 your people held Manchuria virtually as a colony, didn't they? You're Russian, aren't you?"

Her eyes clouded and she nodded with a hopeless, sad look which I had seen on the faces of other *émigrés* when their lost country was mentioned. "I thought so," I continued. "Well, no one objected when your Tsar controlled Manchuria; why should we object when Japan does? It's against the laws of fact to keep eighty million Japanese on a few small islands. If Japan is strong enough to run it, why shouldn't she run Manchuria?"

She nodded and it seemed to me that my answer relieved some doubt in her. "You know a great deal of history," she remarked, "don't you, Casey Lee?"

I finished my third drink before I answered, and my answer made me pleased with my own astuteness. "I know enough about history," I said, "to understand that God and justice are on the side of the heaviest artillery." And then I stopped. "Hello," I said, "what's that?"

But I knew what the sound was. I was only asking the significance of the sound at that particular time and place. I had heard it on the Piava and in the Balkans and in Africa — the sudden thumping of a drum and the cadence of feet on a pavement — hundreds and hundreds of feet moving in unison of infantry — well-disciplined, sedulously drilled infantry. Outside of the hotel I knew that there must be at least two companies of Japanese soldiers, — short, muscular boys with conscientious, half-worried faces, in neatly fitting khaki uniforms with rifles and shining bayonets. The beat of a drum and marching feet was a common sound in Tokio.

She understood my question. "The Manchukuo envoys are coming back from their audience," she said, and then she rose. "Have you had enough to drink before lunch?" she inquired politely. "It seems to me you have. Perhaps we'd better go."

Once I was on my feet, I felt the effect of my three double whiskies. I felt comfortable and nonchalant and friendly with the world, aware that people were looking at me, aware that I was walking beside the best-looking girl in the hotel.

"Wait!" I heard Sonya say beside me. "The party is coming in."

The steps to the hotel door were lined with officers and government officials, each one of whom seemed to know his place. I was tall enough to look over their heads. An old Chinese gentleman was walking up the steps, straight and active, though he must have been well in his seventies. He wore the long black gown of China with a blue vest over it. His face was a scholar's, benign and calm.

"It is Premier Cheng of Manchukuo," I heard Sonya say. "He has followed the Emperor Pu Yi through his exile."

The old man, rising tall and a little bent above his escort of Japanese, seemed to me to have more dignity than anyone in that gathering. His native dress stood out, simple and suitable among the Europeanized uniforms and the cutaway coats and silk hats. He was the only one who seemed genuine — a man with an ideal who looked a trifle sad. I moved toward the door again.

"Wait," said Sonya, "you cannot go out now."

"Why not?" I asked and began to push my way through the crowd.

"Wait!" said Sonya again more sharply.

But before I heard her, I had shoved against a

man in khaki uniform who turned around quickly. I saw by his insignia that he was a captain of cavalry. A short man, with a square copper-colored face.

"No, no!" he said and pushed me on the chest.

Before I thought of the consequences, I took him by the shoulders and spun him out of the way. I must have been rougher than I intended, for he gave an indignant cry, and his voice caused half a dozen other officers to gather angrily around me. "Get out of the way!" I said. "I'm going out this door." Then I saw that Sonya was beside me, speaking quickly to one of the officers in Japanese.

She had opened her handbag and was holding a signet ring in her hand which I thought I had seen somewhere before. It came over me abruptly where I had seen it: it had been on Mr. Moto's finger that other afternoon. Either the ring or her explanation had an immediate effect. The officer whom I had treated rudely bowed to me jerkily and Sonya and I walked calmly out the door of the hotel. As we stood in the cool spring air, a motor moved through the porte-cochere, obviously not one of the usual public cabs, but a more expensive car driven by a man in dark livery.

"Get in," said Sonya. "I know a perfect place to go to lunch." And I climbed in beside her. She was speaking in Japanese to the chauffeur, in sharp staccato phrases. Then she leaned back contentedly and I could smell again the perfume of gardenias. She seemed perfectly at home in that car. "We will go to a teahouse," she said, "and have lunch, just you and me."

"Sonya," I said, "you're a very remarkable girl."

"Oh, no," she said, "but I like you, Casey. I think you're very nice."

I did not answer. Whether it was true or not, I was pleased that she liked me, but I still had sense enough to know what she was by then. The ring had told me. It revealed, among other things, that I had never asked her to lunch and that she was a Japanese spy. Not that the idea shocked me. Instead, it pleased me. She was a Japanese spy and I was no one—footloose and entirely on my own, being speeded through Tokio in a limousine.

"Sonya," I said, "I don't care where we're going as long as you come along."

41

She laughed and touched my hand for a moment. "It's beautiful," she said. "Isn't Tokio beautiful in spring?"

I did not answer. As a matter of fact, I did not think that Tokio was wholly beautiful. The new Tokio of the earthquake was entirely European. We were passing the marble façades of buildings which seemed to have been reared yesterday and which might have been part of Europe — as alien to that land as I was. It was a confusing, dreamlike place and the people on the streets seemed to share that confusion in their mixture of Japanese and European clothes. The motors and the tramcars and the bicycles shared it. The people of Tokio seemed trying hard to be something which they were not; and everything was change and chaos — everything except the green parks on the right and the ancient black wall and moat of another age which surrounded the mystery of the Imperial Palace Grounds, where roofs and rock pines jutted out unobtainably against the sky.

"It's beautiful," I said, "as long as you're here, Sonya."

CHAPTER III

THE DRIVE was a long one, through streets of factories and through densely populated sections of crowded wooden bungalows, lightly, impermanently constructed, as though solider homes were not worth building in the face of the earthquakes that so frequently visit those islands. More recent experiments with steel and concrete, such as had risen in that part of Tokio which had been destroyed in the earthquake disaster of 1923, might mean a general rebuilding of Japanese cities; but until this slow process was completed, I could understand Japan's sensitiveness to any enemy threat from the air. A sight of those unpainted matchboxes of dwellings, with hardly air space between them — and our motor moved through street after street — explained why Japan watched with unconcealed misgivings the construction of our airplane carriers and the development of Chinese and Russian aviation. A few incendiary bombs were all that would be needed to bring about almost unimaginable disaster, and I had been told that the inflammability of Osaka and other great industrial nerve centers of the Empire was even more pronounced.

Sonya had told the driver where to go and finally, after perhaps twenty minutes, the car stopped at the entrance to one of those narrow alleys where the Japan of the Shoguns meets the life of a modern aspiring nation.

"We must walk here," she said, as we got out. The alley was a twisting, flagged street which wound between the low façades of shops and houses.

I think those small streets will always be fascinating to a foreigner. They seem perfect and yet so fragile that a gust of wind might blow them out to sea: tiny, sliding, latticed paper windows, balconies with potted dwarf trees standing on them; minute provision and hardware shops, the flash of flowered kimonos and the clatter of wooden shoes. The alley which we traversed seemed as harmless as an illustration in a tale for children. I remember thinking that it had the same naïve quality of

Germany before the war — of something not to be taken wholly seriously.

"Where are we going?" I asked.

Sonya smiled. "Are you impatient walking?" she asked. "It's so pleasant here. You and I seem like something in the book of the English writer named Swift. 'Gulliver's Travels', isn't it? We are going to a teahouse where we can have *sukiaki*. The management is expecting us."

As she finished speaking, she pointed to an unpainted wooden wall of a building larger than the others. "It's here," she said, and she pushed open a gate. Once inside the wall we were in one of those miniature gardens which represent an art so completely mastered by Japan.

Sonya and I were standing, two giants in a countryside where ponds and streams and plains and mountains rose in contours around us hardly ever above the knee. We looked upon dwarfed fir trees, the tallest not above two feet, with green lawns beneath them. Among the mosses by the pools all sorts of small flowering plants were bending over the water, and goldfish were swimming beneath the surface, peculiar breeds of goldfish whose propagation had been carried on through centuries. That small yard gave us all the perspective and vista of a huge garden, all condensed into the space of a European room. A door at the end of the walk had opened already, and three women in kimonos came out, smiling and bowing. Being familiar with the habits of such places, I sat down on the step leading to the house and took off my shoes and thrust my toes into a pair of slippers which one of the girls handed me, while Sonya did the same.

"It's like playing dolls," she said. "Did you ever play dolls, Casey? I used to at Odessa, long ago."

"No," I answered, "only soldiers, Sonya."

"Dolls are better," she said. "We might put on kimonos, do you think?" She spoke to the eldest of the three women, and the two girls brought out kimonos.

I took off my coat and put one on. Then one of the women pattered before us, leading the way along a matting-covered corridor and pushed aside a sliding door, smiling. We both of us kicked off our slippers and entered a private room which was already arranged for us. The furnishings were as simple as a room in ancient Sparta and as fragile as a painting on a fan. A table not more than two feet high was in the center of the room, with a cushion on the floor on either side of it. A charcoal brazier was burning at one end of the table and saucers of meat and chopped green vegetables and soybean oil were standing near it, — the component parts of that informal Japanese dish, as delicious as anything I have ever eaten, called *sukiaki*. At one end of the table, sliding paper windows opened on a balcony that looked out on a similar small garden. Opposite the balcony at the other end of the room there was a recess in the wall that held the only decorations, — a single porcelain figure of a god standing in a teakwood holder with a scroll painting of cherry blossoms behind him. At a lower level in the niche was a vase of flowers meticulously and perfectly arranged according to the careful dictates of the flower art in Japan. That was all; otherwise the room was bare.

I sat on the floor at one side of the table and Sonya sat on the other side. One of the serving girls in her flowered kimono, with her hair done like a Japanese doll's, knelt at the doorway, then bowed and entered and took her place at the charcoal

47

brazier, filling the cooking utensil with the ingredients of the meal. It all made a pleasant sizzling sound of cooking and there was a smell of things to eat above the acrid smell of charcoal. A second girl, kneeling at the foot of the table, placed two tiny cups before us and filled them with hot *sake* wine.

"Here's looking at you, Sonya," I said and tossed off my cup, which the girl refilled immediately. There was a heady quality about that heated wine of Japan. Though it is taken in minute quantities, the cup is always full and one is apt to forget the amount one consumes.

"I hope you like it here," said Sonya.

I told her that I liked it, and I did. Her watchfulness and preoccupation seemed to have left her as she sat there on the floor by the little table. She seemed to have thrown off care with that volatile habit of Russians. She was a hostess who had brought me to a quiet place to be shared by herself and me. Her long lashes half drooped over her violet eyes and her red lips twisted in playful interrogation.

"Why don't you sit here beside me?" I asked.

"Oh, no," she said. "It isn't proper now. Later, perhaps, when the servants leave." We were each handed a green bowl with the yolk of a raw egg in the bottom and then the meal was ready. We reached toward the brazier with chopsticks for bits of the meat and vegetables.

I was aware that a certain pretense between us had been dropped. We had both of us accepted the fact that I had not asked Sonya to lunch but that Sonya had asked me, and she must have understood that I knew well enough that she had asked me for some definite reason. I was perfectly content to watch her and to drink cup after cup of the *sake* wine while I waited for her to lead the conversation. Her first remark was almost banal.

"Here we are," she said, "you and I."

I nodded and answered, "That's my good luck, I think, and I haven't had much luck for quite a while." I saw that she was watching me, but not suspiciously; rather as any woman might watch a man in whom she took an interest.

"It seems strange, doesn't it," she remarked, "that you and I, Casey Lee, should be in this foreign room so far from any place that either of us knows?

It's such a small inoffensive room — don't you think? And yet it represents the culture of two thousand years. It is a part of the beliefs and life of one of the most powerful nations in the world."

"Yes," I said, "go on — if you don't mind my staring at you, Sonya."

"No, I don't mind," she said. "Your eyes are kind. The eyes of most Americans are kind. Your life has been so secure — is that the reason? But there is no security here. Have you felt it? It's a nervous place — Japan."

Her words did not interest me as much as the huskiness in her voice and the lights that kept dancing in her eyes. Her eyes seemed to be asking me wordless questions. Probably we were each wondering about the other as we talked.

"Yes," I said, "Japan is very nervous. Well?"

"Perhaps she has a right to be nervous," she said. "Perhaps it is a state of mind. I wonder. Japan is very proud."

"I don't see what there is to be nervous about," I said.

She laughed.

"Haven't you ever felt that fate, that everything,

was conspiring against you? I've felt that way some-times."

"I wonder if you feel that way now?" I asked her. Her eyes grew hard for a moment. "Never mind about me," she said. "Japan feels that the world is conspiring against her. It makes no difference whether she is right or wrong if she has that convic-tion, and she may be right. On one side of her is the United States — "

"I know," I interrupted. That talk had always made me impatient. "What has the United States ever done to Japan except to pass the Exclusion Act?"

"There are your interests in the Orient," she said.

I had heard enough diplomatic talk in my occa-sional visits to Washington to be familiar with phases of our Pacific relations.

"I know," I answered. "That is a vague term and I've never heard it specified."

"Think of it this way," she said; "think of a great country which is always moving forward — taking. The United States is moving toward Asia — her hand has reached out over Hawaii, over Guam, over the Philippines. Where is she going to stop?"

"I don't know and I don't care," I said. Grotesque as it seemed to be talking to a pretty girl about the affairs of nations, I was curious to see where the conversation would lead us.

"Then on the other side," her voice went on, "on the other side of these little islands is Russia." She was speaking with a feeling that showed me that these matters were real to her. I could not understand why she was concerned when they meant so little to me. "Russia also is always reaching out; Russia was driven from Manchuria at the time of the Czar, but perhaps she is moving back again. They are double-tracking the Trans-Siberian Railway. Vladivostok is a fortress. There are great military bases along the frontier. Russia has stretched out her hand until she holds Outer Mongolia as a buffer State. Where will she go next? — That's what they're wondering in Japan. If you were a Japanese — " She looked at me and stopped.

"I'd be upset," I said. "Is that what you want me to say?"

"I don't want you to say anything," she answered. "I want you to see how certain people feel. The world, through the League of Nations, has repudiated certain political bets of Japan. She has suffered, like all the other nations, from the economic depression. It is not hard to see why a Japanese must feel surrounded. China dislikes and fears Japan. China is building an air force and Japan is vulnerable from the air. Do you blame the average Japanese if he feels hemmed in?"

"No," I answered, "I don't blame him."

"Neither do I." Sonya's voice grew softer. "He looks to the east and seems to see the gray wall of the American battle fleet. He looks to the west and seems to see the Russian army and the Russian air force. And China. Mongolia is full of agents, Harbin is full of spies. He is unhappy — he is restless. The thing which makes him unhappiest is that he has not the understanding and the approval of other nations. I'm sorry for Japan."

"Perhaps they've got themselves too much on their own minds," I said.

"Perhaps," she answered. "But so have you. I seem to have known you for a long while, Casey Lee."

"That's nice," I said.

I had a sudden desire to end this general conversation, though I knew it would have been wiser to have waited. "Have you seen my *dossier*?" I asked.

"Your *dossier*?" She smiled again. "How should I see that?"

And I smiled back. "Because Japan is a suspicious country," I explained. "Every foreigner is thoroughly investigated by the secret police. I can imagine what my *dossier* says, Sonya. 'Casey Lee, a former American naval aviator, and a free-lance air fighter in little wars, who publicly expressed his discontent with his own country. A drunkard, discredited.'. . . Why don't we get down to business, Sonya?" She did not smile when I had finished.

"Business," she said. "All right. May I ask you a question, Casey Lee? You have fought under other flags, your nationality does not tie you particularly. Am I right?"

"Dead right," I said, and drank another cup of *sake*. "So you were sent to sound me out?"

She nodded simply.

"Because I would talk more freely to a pretty girl?" I suggested.

She nodded again.

54

"It's true," she agreed. "The word has come that the people in America will not pay for your transpacific flight. There are certain persons here — never mind who — who wish to ask you a question. Would you fly the Pacific in a Japanese plane — and let Japan have the credit?"

She must have known before I spoke what my answer would be. It seemed to me like the chance of a lifetime. I would have my own revenge if I succeeded.

"Sonya," I said, "for the last hour I've wanted to kiss you, but even if I hadn't, I'd want to now. If you can get me a plane, if you can give me this chance, I'll do anything in the world for you — anything at all." I could see her looking at me with the same expression of pleasure that I have seen a player wear when he has finished a game successfully.

She knew she had me then. We were no longer people but abstractions. Her voice was cool, almost businesslike, as though she said, "Very well, I do not have to bother with you any more." But instead she said:

"Will you please wait here," and she rose from

her cushion on the floor, tall, lithe and straight, and moved toward the little sliding door.

I rose also from my cushion beside the little table, becoming aware as I did so that a foreigner was not fitted for dining in the Japanese manner. The joints of my knees and ankles were stiff from my unaccustomed posture, so that I was glad to stretch myself. It could not have been more than three minutes later when the door slid open. I was not greatly surprised to see my friend Mr. Moto exactly as I had remembered him, with his Prussian-cut hair, cutaway coat and somber studious eyes.

Sonya had evidently given him back the ring, for it was again on his finger just as it had been the previous afternoon. He smiled, bowed and drew in his breath between his teeth. I wished that I could imitate the perfection of the Japanese bow where the head drops forward suddenly as though a knife had severed the spinal cord and then snaps back upright.

"Mr. Moto," I said.

"You remember me, then?" said Mr. Moto. "That is kind of you, when I thought you might have forgotten. I am so glad to see you here."

My gaze seemed to glance off the smoothness of the little man's determined courtesy. "The pleasure is all mine," I said.

"I can well understand," he answered. "Miss Sonya is so charming. I am pleased that you have both come to understand each other. A very remarkable girl."

"Where is she now?" I asked.

Mr. Moto smiled again. "She will be back," he replied; "have no fear. But first I wish to speak to you alone. I represent a group, if you understand me, that has been seeking for someone to fly the Pacific in a Japanese-made plane. You would not object, I hope, to taking our side in a friendly rivalry between Japan and the United States."

"You show me the plane," I said, "and I'll thank you to the end of my days. I'm a good pilot, Mr. Moto."

"There is no need to discuss your qualifications," he said. "I know very well you are."

"I thought you did," I answered.

"If you had been born in Nippon," Mr. Moto's voice was slow and careful, "I think you might have had more consideration. America is so large and powerful that she forgets more easily than we do, I think."

I knew that he was referring to my wild talk at the hotel. I shrugged my shoulders.

"Without discussing my feelings," I told him, "I can tell you frankly that my nationalistic sentiments will not interfere with my flying a Japanese plane, or even working in some other way. I cannot see how there is anything more than friendly rivalry between Japan and America."

Mr. Moto looked at me enigmatically. There is a nameless something in a man, whether he is Asiatic or European, which raises him above the average and I knew that Mr. Moto had that attribute. Neither of us had committed ourselves in a single detail and yet Mr. Moto seemed satisfied with my answers. He even seemed entirely familiar with my thoughts and sympathetic with my situation. "You interest me," he said softly. "Would you mind explaining yourself?"

"What I mean," I replied, "is the event of war. Both our countries have discussed it, but I do not see the possibility of war between us. I think that possibility was over when the United States gave up using the Philippines as a large naval base. The United States has no means of attacking you. While the Hawaiian Islands are under the American flag, it is nearly impossible for you to reach the coast of North America. With the Japan sea, a Japanese lake, and with your present naval building program, I see no chance for an American fleet to approach Japan. Sensible men discount war talk, I think, Mr. Moto."

My speech appeared to please him. "I am so glad," he said. "I can only say that I agree with you heartily. You are a sensible man, Mr. Lee. Shall we have a drink together? Whiskysoda, eh? American whiskysoda for good Japanese and good Americans."

He walked to the door in his stocking feet and called out an order to a servant and a minute later we were sitting down at the small table with our drinks.

I drank mine quickly and filled my glass again, but Mr. Moto consumed his in small careful sips, like a man who had no faith in his alcoholic capacity. I felt the time had come for us to be frank with each other.

"Mr. Moto," I said, "you have found me at a time of great misfortune. I am under no illusions why you are interested in me. You probably heard something I said yesterday at the hotel. I am not prepared to retract any of my remarks. If the opportunity you offer me is genuine, I shall do a good deal to earn it. I imagine I'm close to being an internationalist, Mr. Moto. I know that you don't offer that opportunity for nothing. What is it that you want?"

He did not reply for a while. Instead he looked at the vase of flowers in the niche along the other wall.

"I am very glad to be direct," he said. "I do want something — nothing that will hurt your conscience, I think. You know a good many naval men in your country's fleet. They're friends of yours. You can meet — " he looked at my half-empty glass thoughtfully — "and drink with them, Mr. Lee. They might talk more freely with you than with one of my own countrymen. You follow me?"

"Yes," I said, and I had a curious sensation in my spine as the end of our conversation became more obvious. The little room with its flowers and porcelain figure had assumed in my imagination an ominous aspect. I had a very definite though indefinable sense of personal danger. It was not attributable to Mr. Moto, who sat there in a conscientious parody of a European negotiator. It seemed rather to lie in the bare paper-like walls of that room. There was no disturbing sound, nothing; and yet I was willing to wager that had I started up to leave that room just then I should not have been allowed beyond the door.

"I follow you so far," I said, "but you'll have to go farther, Mr. Moto."

"Gladly," he replied, "as long as you're thoroughly willing."

I knew that he was conveying half a warning, half a threat, but I was willing.

"I understand you, I think," I said.

"Yes," Mr. Moto nodded, "yes, I think you do, so I may be correspondingly frank. A paper, a plan, to be exact, has been abstracted from our naval archives. It is probably now in the hands of some power. My government is simply anxious to learn what power. If you can find out for me that the United States navy is familiar with the plans of a certain new type of Japanese battleship, that is all I wish of you. Do you understand?"

"Yes," I said, and I felt relieved. "I see no real harm in that. You'd find out sooner or later."

"Exactly so." Mr. Moto also looked relieved. "It is a harmless commission. I should not strain your loyalty by giving you a greater one. As a matter of fact, we shall be pleased if your government has this. We fear other powers more. I am being quite open with you. I hope that you agree."

"Very well," I said, "I'll do anything I can." The request seemed harmless enough, but I had an idea that it would have been dangerous if I had refused, and Mr. Moto's next words, distinct and devoid of tone or emphasis, convinced me I was right.

"I am very glad," he said. "You will obey orders then?"

"Yes," I said, "I can mind orders."

"I am very glad," Mr. Moto said again. "I am afraid, Mr. Lee, you must obey them, now that we've gone as far as this. No one would be greatly surprised if you were to disappear — would they, Mr. Lee?"

"Is that a threat or a promise?" I asked.

He paused a moment before he replied.

"I will leave the answer to your own intelligence. When you get back to the hotel you will find a ticket in your room for the *Imoto Maru,* which sails from Yokohama to Shanghai tomorrow night. You will be given ample money for expenses. You will simply mix with the colony of your countrymen in Shanghai — particularly naval officers. There will be further instructions for you later. You understand, I hope."

"Yes," I said, "I understand. And it's understood I have a plane to fly the Pacific when this job is over."

Mr. Moto nodded and held out his hand. "That is entirely understood, and now, I am so glad to have met you. Miss Sonya will see you back to your hotel. There must be no mistakes." There was something in Mr. Moto's manner that showed me there must be no mistakes.

My opinion was confirmed when he slid open the door and I saw several men lounging in the narrow hall outside. A minute later Sonya and I were walking up the narrow street and at its end the same car was waiting for us. Though she was beside me, I had never felt so completely friendless or so cut off from everything I had known. The business I had accepted, though not wholly creditable, seemed harmless enough, particularly when the reward was considered; yet I wondered — was it harmless? Sonya walked beside me, humming a little tune, strange and wild — some Russian peasant song.

"There is one thing," she said, when we were seated together in the automobile. "You must recognize no one on the boat."

"Very well," I answered. Her eyes were on me curiously. She was looking at me soberly and somehow she seemed dangerously competent. I could imagine that she had an automatic pistol in the white handbag on her lap.

"Any other orders?" I asked.

"No," she said, "not now. So you are one of us, Casey Lee. We are both without a country now." Her words were like the slamming of a door. All my past seemed to be definitely closed and definitely behind me.

I was aware in some way that I had sold part of my soul. I did not mind just then, so long as I was getting value for it. "It is flattering that they have set you to watch me, Sonya," I said. "You're a pretty nurse. Shall I call you nurse?"

"You're right," she answered. "I'm watching you."

"Sonya," I asked her suddenly, almost involuntarily, "what are you getting out of this?"

"Never mind." Her eyes were hard. "I'm being paid a price. You'll do well not to ask questions after this. Simply obey orders, Casey Lee."

I looked at her. Her figure beneath her tailored dress was lithe and strong. Her long fingers were strong and capable. "You're a pretty nurse," I said, "but I'm sorry you're a nurse."

"Let that be as it may." Her throaty voice tinkled like ice in a glass. "We're only even. I'm sorry you're what you are."

"We've got that much in common," I answered cheerfully. "I guess we neither of us have much to boast about, but we're professionals, Sonya. We can earn our pay."

I have tried to set down an accurate and unbiased record of these scenes, without a single effort to put myself or my motives in a favorable light. I wish emphatically to affirm that I meant **every word**

65

which I said to Moto, that I entered in good faith into a contract which doubtless would seem shocking to many of my fellow citizens. The only reason I can conscientiously offer for my conduct is a humble one, not valid in any court of law — that I did not understand. I did not understand, until subsequent events forced the comprehension upon me, how strong the ties of nationality and race become, when they are presented clearly. There is no quibbling with those ties; there is no way of rationalizing them, when events force one to make an actual decision. I was faced with that decision sooner than I expected — on the very night, in fact, when I boarded the *Imoto Maru*, which reminds me that I am writing a record that has no room in it for moralization. I had better get on with my report, only pausing for one addition. Men die for their faith who have never been inside a church, and men die for their country, although they may have spent their lives criticizing all its works. The amazing thing about it is that they are probably surprised by their irrational willingness to die.

CHAPTER IV

Half an hour after I was aboard, the *Imoto Maru* had moved from the dock in Yokohama and was slipping past the harbor lights of that great port into the Pacific, on her way along the Japan coast to China. She was taking me on a trail which was entirely new to me, for aside from those useless weeks of waiting in Tokio I had never seen the Orient. I had a comfortable sensation of excitement such as one has nearly always when a ship carries one into the dark. There is always a sense of the unknown in the darkness which may be inherited from the dread of ancient mariners who thought their ship might slip off the end of the world into space. From my point of view the simile was almost true. The *Imoto Maru* had carried me off the edge of my world, it seemed to me beyond hope of returning. I did not mind it very much.

First I took a turn around the first-class quarters

of the ship. The *Imoto* was small, as liners go now-adays. Except for her swarthy, stocky-looking crew, she reminded me of the transport which had carried me to France in another incarnation. Companion steps led from the promenade deck down to the bow and the cargo hatches and I climbed down, as there seemed to be no restriction, and walked past the battened hatches and hoisting gear out toward the bow itself. Everything ahead was black except the water beside our hull, which was so brilliantly phosporescent that evening that it glowed and flashed into flame.

Suddenly it came over me, without my being able to analyze the reason, that I had been followed ever since I had been on that boat. I turned and stared into the dark shadows of derricks and ventilators but I could see no one. Then I felt in the side pocket of my coat for my leather-covered flask and took a drink. It occurred to me that the time had come to do some serious thinking, but the drink from the flask made me delay it, and instead, I thought of Sonya. I wondered if I would ever see her again. Probably not, I decided, for one who has led my sort of life becomes used to inconsequent shifts of personalities. Still, I was sorry that she had left me, and the poignancy of my sorrow surprised me and filled me with a desire to see lights and people, a desire which led me aft to the smoking room.

The *Imoto,* as I have said, was a small ship and the smoking room was a small cabin done in the dull, dark wood decorations of smoking rooms the world over. Japanese and Chinese business men were seated about the little tables, reminding me that the Orient was fast becoming like the rest of the world and that manners and customs were superficially, at any rate, becoming nearly the same in every part of it. At first I thought I was the only European there until I heard someone calling me. A small, hard-bitten, sandy-haired man was waving a glass at me from the other end of the room.

"Has the liquor got me at last," he whooped, "or is that you, Casey Lee?"

Then I knew how small the world was and how strangely paths become crossed. A picture of the sandy hair, and the sandpaper-like features flashed across my mind, though I had not seen them for a long while. The man was one of those wanderers like myself; Sam Bloom, an old pilot from one of the army squadrons who had come into my life during the war and who had disappeared almost as casually. At another time I should have been glad to have seen him, for there is a companionship among flying men which time does not efface, but just then I was almost embarrassed. How was I to explain to Sam Bloom exactly what I was doing? Far from feeling my embarrassment, Sam gave another whoop of delight.

"Come on, Casey!" he shouted. "Come over here and we'll drink out the bar!"

"Sam," I said, "let's get out of here," and I took him by the scruff of the neck and yanked him out the door onto the deck.

"Hey," said Sam Bloom.

I got a firmer grip on his coat collar. "Come down to my cabin," I said. "We can talk better down there."

Bloom's topaz-colored eyes grew alert. "Anything the matter, Casey? What are you doing here?"

I did not answer him until we were in my cabin, an outside room on B deck, on an aisle amidship. The cabin was big enough to show that Mr. Moto had done me well. A large bed, two upholstered armchairs, a wardrobe closet.

"Say," Bloom said, "you're living in style, aren't you, Casey? Well, you're in the big money now."

"I'm not," I said. "The Pacific flight's all off. I'm going to Shanghai."

"Is that so?" said Sam Bloom, and for the first time in our conversation, his voice had turned cautious. "If you're looking for a job—" He eyed me and tapped a cigarette against the back of his hand. "You're able to take a job, aren't you, Casey?"

"What makes you think I'm not?" I asked.

"You're looking seedy," he said. "Your fingers shake. Listen, Lee, it wouldn't make me popular if I said it out loud here on a Japanese boat, but I'm a flying instructor for the Chinese army. Say the word and I'll get you in."

I was embarrassed as to how to answer.

"Maybe—I don't know," I said.

We must have talked there about old times for an hour, and when he left me I felt bitterer than usual. Bitterer because Sam Bloom also had pitied me, and out of the kindness of his heart had offered me the only opportunity he could think of, the

71

chance of teaching young Chinese soldiers how to fly. I almost wished that he had offered me that chance a day before, because I think I would have taken it gladly, but it was too late now. Then another thought struck me.

No one had asked me for my tickets or my passport — a strange omission for a passenger vessel — and how was I to land in China?

It had not occurred to me until that moment that I had torn my passport in two and had thrown it on the floor of the Imperial Hotel at Tokio. I reached automatically for my inside pocket that contained the envelope with my steamship tickets. I had not examined them carefully before, but now that I did so, I was confronted by an astonishing sight. In the envelope beside the tickets was my passport, so perfectly mended that I could hardly detect a break in its pages. The sight of it reminded me that Mr. Moto had thought of everything.

The engines of that ship were pulsing beneath me, sending a steady throbbing tremor up and down my spine. That restless feeling of vibration reminded me again that I was being carried to an unknown place on an incomprehensible errand. The knowledge made me feel distinctly ill at ease and the uncertainty made me restless. My wrist watch told me that it was late, already close to midnight, but I had no desire to sleep. Instead, I walked back through the companionways and up the stairs to the smoking room. That was when I had my first shock of surprise, just as I stood on the threshold of that small and rather ugly room.

The passengers had cleared out by then, except for a Japanese in a cutaway coat and a woman with reddish-gold hair, who was seated with him at one of the round tables. At first I thought that I was dreaming, but there was no mistake as to who those two were. Mr. Moto and Sonya Karaloff, whom I had believed I had left permanently in Tokio, were there in the smoking room, talking in low voices. In my astonishment I found it difficult to analyze my feelings, but I experienced something like a twinge of jealousy when I saw that girl with Moto at the table.

"Why, hello," I said. "I thought I was here alone."

It was a silly enough remark, as I knew I had not really been alone since Moto had clapped eyes on me at the Imperial Hotel. I knew that I had been watched carefully ever since. But their reaction was amazing.

Mr. Moto turned toward me politely and raised his delicate eyebrows so that his forehead puckered in wrinkles up to the shoebrush cut of his black hair.

"Excuse me," he said, "there must be some mistake."

"What?" I asked him. "What mistake?"

He smiled apologetically. "It is so easy for a foreigner to mistake one of my people for someone else," he said. "I am so very sorry. I have never had the pleasure — of meeting you before."

Sonya was looking at me also, blankly, half amused. "Nor I either," she said. "There must be some mistake."

I gazed at them stupidly before I remembered Sonya's cautioning me that I was not to recognize anyone on the boat.

"I beg your pardon," I said then. "This was careless of me."

Mr. Moto smiled tranquilly and answered, "It is quite all right, but it is better to be careful."

That was all there was to the scene. We did not say another word and perhaps there should have been no need for anything further to convince me that I was in the midst of something that was dark and devious, almost sinister — not after seeing those two there.

I sat in the corner of the smoking room for a little while as though I were a stranger, watching Sonya and Moto from the corner of my eye. I did not like it. I did not like to see her sitting with Moto, though it was none of my business. I felt that she did not belong in such a rôle. Finally I rose and went on deck. There was nothing but a warm breeze and a dark sea on deck, but, all the same, although the promenade seemed deserted, I had that same feeling of being watched. I could have sworn there were footsteps behind me as I walked by the rail. Once I was so sure of it that I spun around sharply on my heel, only to discover that there was no one visible — only the bare promenade behind me with a row of electric lights above it. Finally I went to my stateroom again, not because I wished to sleep, but because the place, on account of my baggage, was familiar and reassuring.

The cabin was just as I had left it, with my bags in exactly the places I remembered, but in some way I knew that someone had been there in my absence. Perhaps everyone, some time in his life, has had a similar experience of awareness — nothing else. As soon as I turned to bolt my door, I knew that my intuition was right, for the bolt had been removed. I could see the holes where the screws had been driven into the white woodwork of the door, but there was no bolt, and the sight gave me a second idea. I reached for my large leather suitcase and began fumbling with the straps, hastily and rather clumsily. If there was no bolt on the door, at least I wanted to be armed.

I had travelled in Japan with a thirty-eight automatic. I cannot remember exactly why I had taken this precaution, except that the Orient had always seemed a distant and peculiar place. I had carried it in my pocket through the customs and then had deposited it in the bottom of my bag. When I looked for it that night, however, it was not there. For a moment I stood with my hand close to the steward's call button before common sense came back to me. They might not have wished me to lock myself in and they might have abstracted my automatic, but this was probably a part of the meticulous caution of a suspicious race which, I decided, probably meant no harm. Half an hour later I was in bed and had turned out the light. The porthole was open and a breeze blew across the cabin and I lay for a while listening to the swish of water and the throbbing of the engines before I went to sleep.

I have never been sure of the time when I woke up. It must have been in the dark of the small hours of the morning when something caused me to open my eyes, only to find myself staring into the black; but a flyer's life makes the senses quick to perceive changes of atmosphere which may not dawn on others who have passed quieter days. As soon as I opened my eyes, I knew there was something wrong in spite of the same steady pulsing of the engines, and the same sound of water. Yet there was some change in the darkness which I could not describe. I knew I was not alone in my cabin. The knowledge did not frighten me as much as it annoyed me, for I was growing tired of constant espionage.

"Who's there?" I said.

A voice answered, so close to my ear that I gave a start. Though I could not see a thing, I knew that whoever was there must be kneeling beside my bed.

"Hush!" It was a man's voice, speaking very softly. "Please do not speak loud. I am a friend, Mr. Gentleman! I do not hurt."

"Who are you?" I asked. Something in his voice made me careful not to raise my own. "What are you doing in here?"

"Please—" the voice was nearer to me—"don't turn on the light! I do not wish them to see light. It is very dangerous, so many watch."

I reached down and grasped an arm of the man beside me. "Who are you?" I demanded again. "What do you want?"

"Only to speak to you." The answer came again, so softly that I had difficulty in catching the words. The arm did not move away. The impassiveness of that arm more than the voice made me listen. "Please do not speak loud or turn on the light. I'm in very great danger, Mr. Gentleman. I come and no one see, I think. I go and no one must see. I have something which they want. You are an

American—you know American navy men."

"Well," I said, "what of it?"

"You know an American navy gentleman they call Commander Driscoll? You see him. You tell him I come to you. You tell him Ma come. I am in great danger, Mr. Gentleman. I think they know who I am. Mr. Moto, he know, I think. Will you tell Commander Driscoll, please—"

"Tell him what?" I whispered, and I knew that the man beside me was afraid of something—deathly afraid.

"I leave you note," he said, "tomorrow, not now. I see you again tomorrow night because you are American. If I die, you tell Mr. Wu Lai-fu in Shanghai, if you please. You give note to him, if Commander Driscoll is not there."

"What are you talking about?" I whispered.

"Please," the voice was trembling in a strange appeal, "I have no time to say. Great danger. If I give you note, you take it, please."

"Why?" I asked.

"Because," the voice seemed closer to me, "because you are American gentleman. Americans all very good people. You see when you get note. You give Driscoll. You tell Wu Lai-fu. Please, I'm going now."

For a moment I lay there, wondering if I were asleep or awake, wondering if I were going mad; then I moved quickly and switched on the light. My cabin door was just closing very softly and there was no one in the cabin.

I could have believed that I had been asleep if it had not been for the sight of that softly closing door. Those whispered words in my ear were exactly like the words spoken by some agency in the subconscious mind which ring in one's memory sometimes when one awakes suddenly and inexplicably in the middle of the night. That closing door was all which proved to me that I had not been asleep. I had been wide awake, listening to mysterious, dreamlike words spoken by a man whom I had not seen. Even though I could not understand those words, I had sense enough to see that they were ominous. They and my nerves conveyed to me the impression that a drama on that Japanese ship was moving silently around me and that I was being drawn into it whether I wished it or not. It was the first time, I think, that I had any definite idea of the seriousness of my own position.

As I tried to set my mind in motion to recall what I had heard, I grew uncomfortably aware that I could not be sure of myself, that my recollections and logic were blurred by alcohol and sleep. I was ashamed to admit to myself that my condition made me unfit to play a definite part in a crisis. Nevertheless, I did the best I could by trying to recall just what had passed. An unseen man, an Oriental, by his voice, who said his name was Ma, had been kneeling by my bed. He had spoken like a man who had been followed and watched; like a man laboring under fear. He had alluded to his imminent danger and to some message which he wished me to convey to Commander Driscoll. He had mentioned the name of a Chinese in Shanghai, and for some reason that name stuck peculiarly in my memory, perhaps because of its phonetic quality — Wu Lai-fu. But what was it about? What business was developing on that ship? What was Moto doing there, or Sonya? Why had the lock been removed from my door and my baggage searched? It was all entirely beyond me, but I felt that my heart

81

was beating fast. I felt that I needed a drink and reached toward my old leather-covered flask which stood on the washstand. I reached for it and then I stopped. For the first time in years my own caution stopped me, for something warned me that my mind needed to be steady — steady without the relaxing effect of alcohol. So, though my nerves were jangling, I did not touch the flask. As I look back, I can always believe that night was a turning point in my career. My life had made me used to excitement and it had also made me reasonable. I was fully aware that it would have been useless and even dangerous to have raised an alarm. Instead of calling, I switched out the light then and got back into bed, not that I could have slept if I'd tried. Nor did I have the slightest desire to sleep, for I had an idea that the invisible stranger might be back again.

If so, I wished to be ready, therefore I half sat up, waiting in the dark, listening to the waves and wind outside my porthole singing that ceaseless song of the sea. There was no way of telling the time, but I must have been there for quite a while before I knew that I was right. Someone was entering my cabin again.

There was no sound of footsteps to warn me, but simply the noiseless opening of the unbolted door, showing first a crack of light from the alleyway outside, a crack which grew appreciably wider. Then, as I saw the light blotted out by a shadow, I slipped noiselessly off my bed. I was able to cross the cabin almost at a single leap and an instant later I was grappling with that shadow. Physical contact gave me a sense of reality. There was a moment's noiseless struggle but whoever I had my hands on was not so strong as I. I could feel heavy woolen cloth and hear a sharp hissing breath. It is hard, at such a time as that, to remember just what happened, but suddenly the cabin light went on without my being able to recall which of us touched the switch. I could only recall that suddenly the light was on and that I was standing in the middle of the cabin, holding a Japanese ship's officer by the throat and shaking him so that he choked.

"Please," the man was saying, "excuse—"

And then I let him go. I let him go but I placed myself between him and the door and slammed it shut, while he stood in the center of the cabin feeling of his windpipe.

"Excuse," he said. "Excuse."

I examined him for a moment before I answered. He was a small man with a face which reminded me of toy breeds of bulldogs which I'd seen at home. Even in that instant, however, there was one thing I was certain of intuitively. He was not the man who had been kneeling beside my bed, because he was not frightened. This little bulldog man had the assurance of a hunter and a bravery incommensurate with his size.

"Excuse," he said again.

"Next time you come in here, knock!" I said. "What's the big idea?"

He began to bow, bobbing his head like a character in Gilbert and Sullivan and raising his hand politely in front of his lips. "It was a mistake," he said. "I am so very, very sorry."

"You're all of you so very, very sorry," I said. "Suppose you answer my question. What brought you inside my cabin?"

He was looking carefully about the room with his square jaw thrust forward, but finally he smiled at me in a bland mirthless way. "There is some mistake," he explained. But obviously something puzzled him. "I thought there was someone else here. Excuse — was there not someone else?"

Some instinct prompted me to lie before I had a definite reason for my motive. It had something to do with the other's face which, in spite of the worry and embarrassment on it, looked relentless.

"What do you mean?" I asked. "Why should anyone else be here? I have this cabin to myself."

Then he straightened himself officially. "I must explain," he answered. "It was my duty. I found myself called away. My duty was to watch your door. I have done very badly. If no one was here, I am very glad."

"No one was here," I said. His narrow eyes bored sharply into mine. Then he glanced about the cabin again.

"You are sure no one has been here and left something? It is important, please."

"No," I said again, "no one has been here."

His eyes concentrated on me keenly, as if something in my manner did not entirely satisfy him.

"Why were you watching my cabin?" I asked.

"Please," he answered, "for your own safety. If no one was here, I am very glad." He bowed again and started toward the door, and I opened the door and let him out.

"Don't come in here again," I said.

"No," he answered, "no, I will not come in again. Please excuse. Good night."

When he was gone, I pushed an armchair against the door. I knew there would have been no use in asking further questions. Nevertheless, one thing was very clear: he had not been there to watch me but to watch someone else. He had not watched sharply enough, and in the space of time when his vigilance had relaxed, someone had entered my cabin. It was as though my room were a trap and as though I were a bait for someone. I knew that the bolt had been removed from my door so that someone could enter my cabin. — Why? I could not answer.

Curiously, however, none of these speculations or events impressed me as much as another matter. A single detail had moved me strangely — irrationally, I could almost think. It had to do with the appeal of that invisible stranger who had whispered in my ear. He had appealed to me because, by accident of birth, I was an American, and something inside me which had lain dormant for a long while was struggling to answer that appeal, strongly, mutely, against my reason, my cynicism and self-interest. My nationality had become so important to me, a matter of such deep significance, that I was startled. I had never realized that a place of birth could mean so much, but it was true. My entire point of view was changing, because I had been called an American.

CHAPTER V

I AM trying to set down the events as they occurred. It is not my fault if they sound fantastic. As I look back, the strangest part of that adventure was the impervious tranquillity of the life aboard that ship which moved on with no reference to myself. When I sat with Sam Bloom in the dining saloon at breakfast the next morning, we seemed so like tourists on a pleasant outing that I could almost forget everything which had occurred. The sun shone through the portholes of the dining saloon upon neat white tablecloths and white-coated efficient stewards.

"Did you sleep all right?" Sam Bloom asked.

"Like a top," I said.

"You don't look it," he answered. "Shall we go up topside and have a drink?"

"No, thanks," I said, though I wanted a drink very badly.

Then he made a remark which sounded like a tourist's.

"The Japanese are an amazing people."

I nodded.

"But dangerous," he added. "They're always watching us, they suspect us all the time." He stopped, looking over my shoulder in such a startled way that I followed his glance, to find that the head steward was standing behind my chair.

"Please," he said, "if you are finished, there is a gentleman who wishes to see you."

"Who?" I asked.

"Please," the steward said, "if you have finished."

I rose and followed him out of the dining room, while Sam Bloom watched us curiously. The steward guided me to one of the *de luxe* staterooms on the upper deck.

"Who wants to see me?" I asked again.

The steward did not answer, but tapped softly on the door until a voice answered in Japanese. Then I was in a private sitting room with the door closed behind me, facing my old friend Mr. Moto, who sat behind a little table, sipping a cup of tea.

Mr. Moto, in his cutaway coat, looked immaculate

and composed, and I was glad to see him, for I felt that Mr. Moto owed me an explanation. He waved me to a chair, smiling as he offered me a cigarette.

"Good morning, Mr. Lee," he said. "We may recognize each other in private. Are you quite comfortable? I am so sorry that you did not sleep well last night."

"Thanks," I said, "I didn't. Do you mind if I make a further remark?"

"No," he answered. "Please what remark?"

"I'd like to say," I replied, "that I'm confused."

"Life," Mr. Moto answered, "is often confusing; do you not think?"

I dropped my cigarette into an ash tray, the bottom of which was filled with water.

"Will you have a drink?" Mr. Moto asked. "What? Not drinking? Something must have disturbed you last night."

"One of your officers disturbed me," I said. "I found the bolt was off my door and one of your officers put his head in. Would you care to tell me why?"

It was plain he did not care to tell me why. Instead, he wriggled his shoulders apologetically.

"I have heard," he answered. "Excuse. It was so very careless of the man. His duty was to see that you were not disturbed. He was not true to his duty. Was that the only thing that disturbed you, Mr. Lee? I shall like it if you will tell me."

"Yes," I answered, and I still don't know what induced me to prevaricate except that new national sense of mine. "Only the officer bothered me. Suppose we be frank, Mr. Moto," I added.

"Why not," he answered. "That is what I am here for, yes? You are sure there was no one else in your cabin? It is very important — and so I ask."

"I was drunk last night," I said. The answer must have satisfied him, for I could feel a certain tension relaxing in the room and Mr. Moto sank back in his chair and lighted a cigarette. In the silence that followed, the turgidness of everything began to strain my patience.

"Perhaps," I suggested, "you were expecting someone else to come into my cabin?"

His expression changed at that. To my surprise, I found him looking at me almost with respect. "So. That is so. Yes," he answered. "That is why I wish to speak with you. You can be of very great use to us, Mr. Lee, if you do exactly what I say. I do expect someone to come to your cabin, and if he does, I hope you will ask no questions, no matter what may happen. It is very important — do you understand?"

"Why is it important?" I asked.

Mr. Moto stared thoughtfully at me for a while before replying, his opaque brown eyes devoid of meaning.

"I cannot tell you why it is important," he answered. "I only ask you to do exactly what I say, please. There is someone on this ship whom we desire very much to interrogate. Unfortunately, we have no exact description and do not know who he is. We — ah — guess he is on this vessel, and I hope so much we guess right. We hope that he comes to your cabin. Then, you see, we will know him."

"Why should he come to my cabin?" I asked.

Mr. Moto paused a minute. He gazed at me as if I were a figure in a column of addition, not a person of flesh and blood. "I will be frank," he answered finally; "because you were once an American naval officer he will come. It is nothing that concerns you, if you please. You need not be disturbed. You are not disturbed, are you?"

Though I tried to keep my expression blank, I was very much disturbed. "Any other orders?" I said.

"No," he replied, "not now. Simply amuse yourself, Mr. Lee, and — yes, this: Do not think too much of anything that has happened. There is very good brandy in the smoking room and it is a very nice morning. You must not worry. You do so well and everything goes so nicely." He rose and bowed. "Good morning, Mr. Lee."

I bowed also, and then I found myself outside the door, unpleasantly aware that I was a pawn on Mr. Moto's chessboard, which did not please my egotism, because I have never liked to be a pawn. I had not told Mr. Moto of the visitor to my cabin, and now I knew that nothing would induce me to tell him.

I shall never forget the rest of that day, if only because of its utter lack of incident, for nothing happened, absolutely nothing. The life on that *Maru* steamer simply lowered itself to the routine boredom of shipboard, leaving a passenger like me to his own limited devices. At such a time, to anyone of my temperament, the lack of definite outlet by action was peculiarly appalling. On another occasion I would have relieved the suspense by drink, as I was tempted to do more than once that day. But that desire to keep my mind clear was still uppermost in my thoughts. I paced the deck for a while, looking out to starboard at the blue mountainous coast line of Japan and watching the occasional slatted sails of fishing fleets. I could not blame the Japanese very much for desiring more land; for the islands of the Empire seemed, as one viewed them from the sea, almost entirely composed of jagged mountain slopes which offered little opportunity in the way of life or husbandry. Behind the pastel purples and blues and greens of distant mountain ranges, which seemed to conceal the secrets of Nippon, I could think of a teeming population longing to leave that unstable volcanic coast. The fishing fleet was like a part of that desire pushing out from the mountains to the horizon. Our own ship, with its squat capable sailors, was a part of it. The red-and-white flag of Nippon was pushing out to sea, to end no one knew just where.

As I walked forward and glanced toward the line where the horizon met the sky in soft gray clouds, I saw another sight which made me halt at the rail and stare — an apparition that was half beautiful, half sinister. Out of the cloud bank by the horizon appeared the masts of ships that seemed to have, at that distance, almost the impalpable qualities of clouds. A division of a battle fleet was out on one of its perpetual maneuvers — gray Japanese cruisers moving behind a formation of submarines and destroyers. There was a foreboding quality to that half-visible sight, because I understood, as everyone who has walked a deck of an American warship understands, that Japan's naval strength might some day be directed at my country; that it was reaching out like an arm across the Pacific toward our coasts where our own fleet was watching. There was destiny in the sight, which was a part of the obscure irrational destiny of peoples never to be wholly clarified by reason. It was solitary being on a Japanese ship, the only representative of my country except that casual aviator, Sam Bloom. That situation made me feel very keenly the differences of race, and more aware than I think I ever have been, even in the distant days of the World War, that I was an integral part of my country. Then I heard Sam Bloom speaking to me and I was glad that he had come to stand beside me. I had never been so much drawn to that little sandy-haired friend of mine as I was at that moment, simply because we were strangers among a strange people. I had an impulse to tell him everything which had happened to me. I think I should have, if I had not felt suddenly ashamed of my position and of myself.

"Nice-looking lot of boats, aren't they?" he remarked.

"Yes," I said.

"I wonder if we'll ever fight 'em?" remarked Sam Bloom.

"A lot of people wonder that," I found myself answering, glad to speak to someone who had an intonation like my own. "I hope to heaven we don't. In spite of the arguments about the Japanese never having encountered a first-rate power, I'm afraid they'd make a lot of trouble, Sam."

Sam Bloom squinted his eyes out toward the horizon and drummed his stubby fingers on the rail. "Last time I was in Shanghai, there were a lot of rumors," he said. "The word is, those boys are up to something; that they've hit on some new naval secret. They're clever and persistent. That's the word — persistent. They're getting so that they can beat us at all our manufacturing trade. But we can't stop them, can we? How about a drink?"

"No, thanks," I said. "I'm on the wagon."

I did not blame Sam Bloom for being incredulous.

"Say, Casey, is anything on your mind?" he asked.

"Only myself," I answered, "and that doesn't amount to much."

"Say," said Sam, "there's a pretty girl around here. Did you see her? Reddish-yellow hair. Russian, I suppose. Shanghai is full of white Russians — not that any Europeans meet them socially. Let's go and talk to her. She doesn't look as if she'd mind."

"Try it," I said. "I tried last night." I saw that Sonya was walking toward us down the deck.

"You watch me," said Sam and took off his hat and smiled. "Hello. It's a nice morning!" But Sonya

97

walked by like an alluring figure of the imagination, nothing more.

Those violet eyes of hers stared straight through us. There was a whiff of gardenia scent and she was gone.

"Well," said Sam Bloom. "My mistake. We're not popular on this boat, Casey. How about a drink?"

"You have one," I said.

There is no need to describe any further the events of that day. They rolled by as easily as the ship rolled through an oily sea. A stop at the docks of Kobe. A game of cards, lunch in the small dining saloon, where Japanese passengers ate with chopsticks and made strange noises over their food. Another game of cards in the smoking room, where I watched Sonya and Moto talking at a table near the door.

"So that's the answer," Sam Bloom said. "She's that little swell's mistress — that's the answer."

"That isn't so," I answered, before I thought.

"Say —" Sam Bloom looked at me — "how do you know?"

"I don't believe she is — that's all," I said.

Yes, the day dragged on, a horrible, eventless day.

Dinner in the dining saloon and back in the smoking room again, an interminable walk along the deck and back to the smoking room again. I was waiting for something to happen, but nothing happened. Finally, when Bloom and I were left alone in the smoking room except for two sleepy stewards, I believed that nothing would happen. My lack of sleep the night before began to make me very drowsy and finally I said good night to him. I hope he had a good one.

CHAPTER VI

IN some curious way my mood must have been changed by the dullness of the day until I was lulled by its dullness into bored security. I had no real suspicion that anything would be wrong when I opened my cabin door. First, when I opened the door, I recall having the distinct impression that I had made a mistake and that the quarters were not mine. Of course, such a sensation as this was only a matter of an instant, which I mention simply to bring out the complete unexpectedness of what I encountered. Subconsciously I knew all the time that it was my cabin, although my common sense told me that it could not be because there on the floor a man was lying face upward — a moon-faced Asiatic man whom I had never seen, dressed in a shoddy suit of European clothes.

He lay on the floor like a drunkard, sprawled out in an attitude of complete abandon and carelessness of convention, shaven-headed, open-eyed, and open-mouthed. For another split second I had a sensation of outrage because I could not understand what he was doing in my cabin overcome by liquor, but the truth manifested itself in an instant. That Asiatic man in the shoddy European clothes was offering his own mute apology for lying face upward on the carpet. A stream of blood, that was making a puddle behind his shoulders, was excuse enough for his seeming rudeness. The man had been stabbed in the back, and not long ago either. But that was not all of the picture. A sound of an indrawn breath made my glance dart from that sight on the floor to the recess near my porthole. Standing there, her face as white as paper except for the paint on her lips, was Sonya Karaloff, holding a knife in her hand.

Anyone who has been through the war is inured to the sight of death. I have seen it, in scores of forms, strike out of nowhere. I have seen dead men mangled by shellfire and dead men lying pallid like men asleep. I have seen the unbelievable liberties which war has taken with the bodies of men, but this present spectacle was different. It was the first time in my life that I had witnessed the scene of cold, premeditated murder, and for a moment it made me sick; and for a moment I felt a wave of nausea rise in me and with the nausea faintness. Then I pulled myself together because, I suppose, my reflexes are unusually quick. Those reflexes were making me move so accurately that they surprised me; even before my mind began to function, I found myself closing the cabin door behind me, not carelessly but very carefully, so that the latch clicked gently. And then, with my eyes on Sonya, I began to speak, without giving way to the horror that was in me. I believe I spoke quite calmly, fortified after the shock was over by my intimate acquaintance with dead men.

"I am sorry," I said. "I'm afraid perhaps I have intruded."

She stared at me, speechless, still holding that knife in her hand, and I noticed that the blade was wet.

"But after all," I said, "this is my room, you know."

And still she did not answer.

Then I found myself making an inane remark. "I

didn't know you were that kind of a girl," I said. "You must be very muscular or surgically inclined. They tell me it isn't easy to stab a man in the back so that he drops right down like this one here."

She opened her lips and closed them — wordlessly.

"It's curious," I said, "the element of time." I found myself continuing simply to steady my own nerves. "If I had been sleepy five minutes sooner, this moon-faced man might still be alive, perhaps. If I had been sleepy five minutes later, I doubt if I should have had the pleasure of having a delightful golden-headed girl like you in my cabin. Which would have been better, I wonder?"

Then, for the first time, she spoke. "It's Ma," she said. "It's Ma — "

Initially the name meant nothing, but then the truth dawned on me. The man I had not seen the night before, the man who had wished to give me something because I was an American, the man who had told me that his name was Ma, was now lying beside my bed, and he would not whisper any more.

"I believe you're right," I said; "it must be Ma."

"You—" she said. She started; a trace of color came into her cheeks; and I saw the pupils in her violet eyes widen. It was not pleasant to see her there in an evening wrap, with a knife in her hand.

"How did you know that?" she asked.

I leaned against the closed door of the cabin but I did not take my eyes off her.

"I think," I suggested, "I should feel more comfortable if you put down that knife. I don't think I've ever struck or mishandled a woman, but believe me I will, if you don't set it down. I don't want my throat cut too."

She looked blankly at the knife she was holding and then she dropped it on the floor. "I did not know I'd picked it up," she said.

"That was very absent-minded," I answered, "don't you think?" Then she moved a step towards me and came near to stumbling over that figure on the floor.

"Please," she said, "please, won't you help me?"

Her suggestion seemed to me grimly amusing—so amusing that I wanted to laugh out loud.

"Don't you think you're very well able to help yourself?" I suggested. "You've done an efficient job — not exactly neat, but efficient. Do you always stab them in the back?"

I do not believe that she heard me. At any rate, she disregarded my question.

Her hand went up to her bare throat, a slim, white trembling hand.

"I — " she stopped and seemed to choke upon her words. "I came here to see you." Again I had an almost uncontrollable desire to break out into laughter.

"That was thoughtful of you," I answered, "but selfishly, perhaps, I am just as glad that I was out." She did not seem to hear me.

"It's Ma — " Her voice was choked. "Don't you see it's Ma?"

"You mistake your tenses," I suggested. "You mean it was Ma, don't you? You Russians are so linguistic that you've conjugated him from the present to the past."

"Don't!" she whispered. "Don't!"

"Oh?" I said. "Perhaps you're sorry, now?"

"Don't!" she whispered again. "Please, please — I didn't kill him! I came to see you. And I found him lying here. It's Ma — "

"So you've said several times," I answered. "Who is Ma?"

By that time she had regained her self-possession. In spite of her delicacy and beauty she always, as I have said, gave one the sense of competence to encounter any situation.

"You don't understand," she said. "I didn't know he was here. Why didn't he speak to me? I suppose he didn't dare."

"Perhaps you didn't give him a chance," I suggested.

"Don't!" She did not raise her voice, but its intensity made me stop. "Don't speak like that! I swear I didn't kill him. You don't understand. He was my father's old interpreter and servant."

Though my intellect told me she would naturally be lying, something made me believe her, for no one could have simulated her look of pain. I thought for a second that she would lose control of herself and weep. Her face became convulsed. She raised a handkerchief to her lips.

"Don't!" I said sharply. "Who killed him then?"

"They —" she whispered. "He must have had a message. They suspected something. Why didn't he tell me?" Then she was completely calm again. Whatever she might have been and whatever she meant, that girl was brave.

If I could not understand what part she was playing in that drama, at least I could admire her bravery. She must have lived a life where one made accurate decisions, without time for much mental debate.

"We must leave here at once," she said. "If he knew I had come here, I don't know what would happen. Please—" she touched my arm and nodded to the door. "Quickly, quickly, please!" Her urgency and the swiftness of her decision made me respond instantly.

I whipped open the door and then we were out in the corridor and her hand on my arm was trembling. There was no one in the passageway.

"This way," she whispered and pulled me around a corner. "Listen! Here they come."

She was right. At the end of the passage we had left I heard soft steps and low voices. If she had not been decisive, they would have seen us in another instant. She snatched at the handle of the cabin door beside us, but even in her haste she was adroit and quick, and fortunately the door was not locked. A second later we were in the dark of a vacant cabin, listening to footsteps and the voices through a crack of the door. Then she closed it noiselessly and we were plunged into pitch blackness, standing close together — so close that I felt her breath on my cheek. She still held my arm and her fingers tightened on my sleeve. I felt her lips brush my cheek as she whispered so faintly that I could hardly hear her.

"I don't think they saw us. You must never say that you came down to your cabin — never! You must wait here for just a moment, not too long. When I open the door, move to the right and go straight up to the deck. Someone will speak to you there, of course. They will say they've changed your cabin."

I whispered back to her and I felt my forehead touch that soft gold hair. "What did you want to see me for? What was it?"

"Because I was a fool," she whispered. "Because I grew to like you. I wanted to tell you something — about this rotten business. I wanted you to be sure you knew what you were doing . . . sure you knew what he was using you for. I can't tell you now because you must go . . . but when you get to Shanghai, go home to America! Go anywhere. Don't trust them! No one should like anyone in this business. I know I've been a fool. Now go quickly up on deck."

"What about you?" I whispered.

"Never mind about me. I know how to look out for myself. Good-by."

But I did not move. I did not want to go away. "I rather like you too," I said. "Will I ever see you again?"

"Probably not," she whispered, and suddenly she threw her arms around me. She held me close to her for an instant. "Good-by — now go!" she said.

I crept through the half-open door and turned to the right as she directed. Except for the vibration of the ship, everything was very quiet. I did exactly what she told me, because I knew she meant every word she said. I hurried up on deck. I could not have been there more than a minute, looking over the rail, when that toy bulldog of an officer came up to me.

"I have been looking for you," he said. "Something has occurred. I am so sorry, if for a few minutes you cannot go to bed."

"Why not?" I asked him. "What's the matter?" And when I asked, I could not help wondering if he was the man who had driven home the knife.

"So sorry," he said apologetically, "so very sorry. The water pipe in your cabin has been leaking. We are removing you to a better one, a *de luxe* cabin on this deck. It will not take long."

"All right," I said. "I never liked that cabin."

"No," he agreed, "it was uncomfortable. A very nice night, is it not?"

They were doing everything very smoothly. Clearly, as a part of the plan, the little officer was there to watch me safe to bed. "It is a nice night," he said again, "is it not?"

"Fine," I answered. "I've been up in the bow. I hope you weren't looking for me long."

"In the bow," he answered; "that is very nice. No, I was not looking for you long."

Five minutes later a steward spoke to the officer softly in Japanese.

"We can go now. Your room is ready," my bull-dog said.

He was right that my quarters were improved. I was shown to a fine cabin with a large square port. My pajamas were laid out, and my slippers and my bags were all in place, in the same order that they had been in the stateroom below. Even my leather-covered pocket flask was standing by the washbowl. Further, to my relief, my cabin door had a bolt on it, which I drew noiselessly as soon as I was alone. Then I looked carefully at my bags and saw that the clothes in them had been moved, although they were folded neatly. My baggage had been searched again. Every one of my pockets had been searched. Every inch of my baggage had been gone over by deft-fingered experts. They had been looking for something in my old cabin. They had been searching for something with a tireless zeal. It was because that dead Chinese had left something there, — some note, some message for me before he had died, a note which he hoped I would give to Commander Driscoll because I had been in the American navy. It must have been an important message, important enough, at any rate, to cost a man his life. I wondered if they had found it. As I wondered, I looked at my pocket flask longingly, for after the excitement, the desire for a drink was very strong in me. I even picked it up and had my fingers on the silver cup that formed the bottom of the flask before I checked myself. I knew more than ever that it would be wise to be cold sober, and I set the flask back in its place.

Then I thought of Sonya Karaloff. I could still feel the touch of her hair against my forehead and the pressure of her arms as she held me close. Had she been sincere at that moment, I wondered? Or was it simply a part of seduction, because she thought I was a broken drunkard who might be used? I could not tell, but I hoped that she had meant it. I was surprised how much I hoped. . . .

I examined the bolt on my door carefully before I undressed for bed, but the bolt was firmly set and I was not disturbed that night. The lock on the inside was perfect, but when I moved back the bolt and endeavored to open the door, I found it had been fastened on the outside also. I was a prisoner in the cabin.

I have never been under any illusion that I'm intellectually brilliant beyond the average. Yet it is true that the shock of such a sequence of events and the realization of imminent danger are calculated either to cause panic or to set the mind at work. They had on me a beneficial effect which was close to a sort of regeneration. They gave me a new perspective on myself.

I knew something which Mr. Moto did not. He was looking for a message and he had not found it, or else he would not have locked my door. Since he had locked me in, he clearly thought that I had found it.

"Let him think," I whispered to myself. "He won't get any change from me."

For I was sure of one thing by then. I was through with Mr. Moto and through with the whole lying devious affair in which he had involved me, and through with all the motives which had drawn me into it. I was myself again. I was Casey Lee. It was a long while since I had been myself.

CHAPTER VII

I DID what I thought was best under the circumstances. I went quietly to bed, confident that I would not remain locked in my room indefinitely; nor was I mistaken. At eight o'clock in the morning there was a tapping on my door, which grew increasingly persistent until I arose and drew back the bolt. It was a room steward carrying a tray with fruit and coffee, and he drew in his breath politely.

"So sorry," he said, "so very sorry. Somehow the door was locked. Please, there is a gentleman to see you." He set the tray on a chair beside my bed.

"Where is he?" I asked.

"Please," the steward said, "if you are ready, he will come right in." He must have taken it for granted that I was ready, because an instant later Mr. Moto appeared in his morning coat.

We must have looked strange, me in my pajamas, and Mr. Moto in his morning coat, but neither of us forgot the formalities. I bowed and Mr. Moto bowed and the steward departed.

"Moto," I asked, "why was I locked in here last night?"

Mr. Moto raised his eyebrows. "I do not understand," he said. "Some mistake, I think." He sat down in a little straight-backed chair near the washstand and lighted a cigarette, and then he said what all his people say continuously: "I am so very sorry. Now I must ask a question. I hope you do not mind."

"Does it make any difference if I mind?" I inquired.

He appeared to consider his answer carefully. "No," he admitted, "perhaps not. What I wish to ask is this — did you visit your cabin last night after dinner?"

"No," I said. "What of it?"

Mr. Moto blew a cloud of cigarette smoke and smiled apologetically. "There is no use lying, Mr. Lee. Please excuse the word."

"Moto," I said, "you shock me."

"I am sorry," Mr. Moto answered, "but were you not in your cabin?"

"You heard me," I said promptly. "I said no."

I wondered if he would speak of what had happened in the cabin and I did not have long to wonder. His opaque brown eyes studied me cryptically for a moment and then he said:

"The knife was moved."

It reminded me of the old days when we sat about a table playing poker, with a heavy pile of chips in the center. I had an idea that Mr. Moto was bluffing, that he was not entirely sure of my movements for about five minutes the night before.

"What knife?" I asked.

Again Mr. Moto considered his answer carefully. "Well," he said, "it makes no difference. You remember our conversation yesterday, Mr. Lee? I have come to get the message."

Then I knew that I had guessed right; they had not found what they had been looking for.

"What message?" I asked.

"There was a message in your cabin," repeated Mr. Moto politely. "It is very important that it should go no further. You have that message, I think."

"Do you?" I asked.

"Yes," said Mr. Moto; "will you give it to me, please?" His tone was considerate. Mr. Moto always was a gentleman.

"I told you," I repeated, "that I haven't got a message."

"I'm so sorry," said Mr. Moto. "If you do not give it to me I shall have to have men in here to search you, Mr. Lee. It will be an indignity that I shall be sorry for. A very careful search of your body. Come — will you give me the message?"

I took a step toward Mr. Moto's straight-backed chair. "Moto," I said, "if you call anyone in here to search me, I'm going to break your neck."

Mr. Moto dropped his cigarette into one of those water-filled ash receivers and reached thoughtfully into his pocket, I believed for his cigarette case, but instead his hand whisked out with a compact little automatic pistol.

"I am so very sorry," he said. "You will stay where you are, Mr. Lee." And he called out in his native tongue. At that exact instant that he called, the door shot open and three stewards filed in silently.

117

"I am so sorry," Mr. Moto said again, "but you must submit to have them search you. Please."

A single glance at the stewards and at Mr. Moto convinced me that any further argument was useless, for the men all had an air of complete efficiency written on them which displayed a familiarity with forms of business not usually practised by steamship employees.

"Very well," I said to Mr. Moto. "You have entirely convinced me."

He did not answer but he smiled most agreeably and put his automatic back into his inside pocket.

If I had not been so personally involved in this search to the extent of losing a good deal of my own dignity, I should have found their procedure interesting. I never really knew until then what was meant by thoroughness. First they went through my bags again, even going so far as to pull out the linings. Then they examined all my clothing and my shoes, shaking, exploring, touching every seam with their fingers. While this was going on, two stewards had the cabin carpets up and the mattress and bedding ripped off to be examined. I will say that they were neat about it. Once they finished, every article was put carefully back in its place. The top of my flask was unscrewed and one of the men probed its contents with a long wire. For easily half an hour the cabin was a vortex of silent, lubricated activity. Each of the men knew exactly what to do, and in case they did not, Mr. Moto made occasional gentle suggestions. Once they had finished with the room, two of them turned to me.

"So sorry," Mr. Moto said, and they stripped off my pajamas, leaving me in a state of nature.

"Like a diamond miner in Kimberly, eh — Mr. Moto?" I suggested.

"Believe me," said Mr. Moto seriously, "what we are looking for is worth more than the Kohinoor, Mr. Lee."

I tried to be indifferent under their prodding fingers and I was somewhat cheered by Mr. Moto's growing air of surprise and discouragement.

"So it is not there," Mr. Moto said. "I am sorry."

"I told you it wasn't there," I answered, "and now do you mind if I put on some clothes?"

"No, indeed." Mr. Moto rose and regarded me seriously. "I am very much afraid that what I am looking for has been destroyed. Can you tell me, Mr. Lee?"

"I can't tell you anything," I answered.

The stewards filed out but Moto paused beside the door. "I am very much afraid," he said, "that what I want rests inside you there." He tapped his wrinkled forehead. "If that is so, you must tell me. You really must. We cannot be good fellows about this matter."

"Why not?" I asked.

"Because what I'm looking for," said Mr. Moto softly, "must not go any further. Will you think this over carefully, please, and someone will be in to talk to you later? I dislike certain parts of my profession very much. Now you must stay here while you think, please." Then Mr. Moto was gone and I heard the lock on the cabin door click softly.

I do not recollect that I was as much alarmed as I was puzzled, not having the slightest idea of exactly what Mr. Moto was looking for. I could not entirely understand why he was so serious, nor did the implications of his remarks immediately dawn upon me. It only seemed to me incredible that a comparatively harmless person like myself, who, a few days ago, had nothing but self to think of, should be caught up in the edges of a completely fantastic snarl. The only thing I could think of by the time I had finished dressing was that I must remain composed.

Now that the door was locked, the air in the cabin seemed still and oppressive and the walls seemed closer together. I walked over to the square porthole and looked out on the shining waters of the ocean, perhaps twenty feet below, but there was no consolation at the sight of that blank sea. Then I tried to open the port, only to discover that it was one of those sliding windows which one screwed down with a cranklike implement which fitted into the sill. That appliance was not there, however. It must have been intentionally removed and there was no way for me to leave that cabin by door or port. It is curious what eccentric matters may disturb one's calm. Nothing upset me as much as that discovery that I could not open my port, that I could not feel the air on my face. It gave me an unreasoning sense of suffocation and panic, which aroused in me a desire to cry out for help, although I knew there was no help and that I must take my medicine. If I had told Moto frankly everything I knew, I might not have been locked inside, but I would be hanged before I would tell him.

It must have been an hour later that I heard the lock of my door snap back with a sound which made my nerves leap strangely. It was not my actual situation but the complete uncertainty of what might happen next that was making me unstrung. Actually the thing that occurred was the last that I expected. The door snapped open and instead of a man that Russian girl came in. She wore a blue dress and a sable scarf hung around her neck. The wind outside had ruffled her hair, making it look as warm and chaotic as fire.

She closed the door carefully before she spoke and stood for a moment watching me with that worldly glance of hers, and I could not tell what she was — a friend or an enemy — from that glance.

"Good morning," she said. "Good morning, Casey Lee."

"I begin to think, Sonya," I said, "that I should be happier if I had never met you. What are you after now?"

"You," she said, but she did not smile.

"How do you mean, me?" I asked.

Sonya shrugged her shoulders. "You ought to understand," she said. "If you can't, please try to think. Why should I be introduced in here? I'm not bad-looking, am I?" Her throaty voice was like her looks — mysterious, alluring. In fact, I had never seen anyone easier to look at and I told her so.

"Well," she said, "don't you see? That's why I'm here. Mr. Moto thought you might be more likely to tell me about what happened to a certain message than anyone else. I think it was rather kind of Mr. Moto, don't you? He's not a brutal man."

"You mean you're here to seduce me?" I inquired.

"You'll be reasonable, now, won't you, Casey dear? It will be so much better. We don't want to be unpleasant. Oh, Casey, please, please, tell me everything you know — " It seemed to me that her voice was unnecessarily loud, before I guessed the reason. She was speaking so that someone outside the door might hear, and her actions were different from her voice, for while she spoke she drew me down beside her on the edge of the bed. "Casey," she whispered, "did they hurt you?"

I shook my head.

"I am thankful," she whispered. "They didn't see me last night. And you didn't tell them. Thank you, Casey."

I did not answer because her actions were entirely beyond me. I did not know whether to suspect her or to trust her. I put my hands on her shoulders and looked hard into her eyes. She returned my glance without faltering.

"What are you here for, Sonya?" I asked.

"The message," she whispered. "There must be some message! I didn't find it. They didn't find it. They think you were down there. Did you find anything, Casey?"

I smiled at her, and my thoughts were very bitter, now that it seemed perfectly clear that she was there to worm something out of me. "You tell Mr. Moto to be damned," I said. "I didn't tell him about you — and I won't tell anything."

"But do you know," she whispered — "do you know anything? You must."

"I guess I'm stubborn!" I said. "I'm not talking, Sonya."

"Casey," she whispered, "please, it isn't that. He

thinks you've memorized the message and destroyed it. If that is so, the message can't go any further. That's why they murdered Ma." She paused and looked at me somberly. "That's why they're not going to let you off this boat alive, because this message can't go any further." Her eyes held my glance, but her eyes revealed nothing. I could not tell whether she was telling the truth nor could I entirely catch her meaning.

"You mean," I inquired, "that I'm going to be locked in here indefinitely?"

She shook her head and the gold in her hair danced in curious rays of light.

"No," she said very softly, "you won't stay on the boat. Your body will be thrown overboard. You will have drowned yourself."

I recoiled from her, edged myself away, and I felt my hands grow cold and my tongue grow thick. There was no use in deceiving myself that I was receiving a hollow threat when I looked at that Russian girl's eyes. There was no use in trying to believe that she was incapable of playing such a part, now that she had spoken. I remembered her in the cabin with the knife, and the memory of that, as much as my own danger, made me sick and dizzy. I was afraid because I was facing the prospect of dying in cold blood, but I was more afraid of her. Pride — for I suppose synthetic heroes are always proud — made me struggle to conceal that fear, made me prefer to die then and there rather than have her know the way I felt and I was determined to tell them nothing.

"So it's murder, is it?" I inquired.

She nodded, as though she found it hard to speak, and I saw her slim white hands clasp and unclasp in her lap.

"Casey dear," she whispered, "you could call it that. I should rather call it a secret agent's life. If you had lived in my country you would know. It's part of the profession. You must not blame them. Don't you see, it's the only thing they can do?"

I cleared my throat because her nearness seemed to choke me.

"Casey," she whispered, "there must be some message. Will you let me read it, please?"

I grinned back at her, or tried to grin, but my lips were stiff and cold and my facial muscles seemed cramped by the effort.

"Sonya," I said. "This business has taught me a good deal. It's taught me that there is still something worth dying for. Go back to your gang and tell them anything you like. Then perhaps you'd like to come back and see that I can die decently. In the meanwhile, if you have any decency, you'd better go away."

I had intended to continue further in saying what I thought of her, but her expression made me stop. She had grown deathly white. She was staring at me as though I had slapped her face.

"Casey," she whispered, "I came here to help you."

"My dear," I answered, "I don't want your help. It's time I learned to help myself. I had nearly forgotten how."

"No," she whispered, "no!" She had pulled the sables from her neck and she was ripping at the lining. "Listen to me! Please, please listen. I have nothing to do with this. I *am* trying to help you. Please, I don't want to see you killed."

"Would it make you any calmer," I inquired, "if I told you I don't believe a word you say?"

She had pulled something from her furs and was

holding it in her hand. A metal crank for the port window.

"Don't you believe me now?" she whispered. "This will turn your window down. Hide it in your bag. They won't search again. They sent me here, but I'm trying to help you, Casey."

I felt the cold metal in my fingers.

"You don't understand," she whispered. "I want that message as much as you. I did not know about it until I saw that it was Ma. I don't want them to have it. They mustn't have it!"

I passed my hand across my forehead and my face was wet and clammy. "What's all this nonsense about?" I demanded. "What is this message?"

She was silent for a moment. "You won't believe me, I suppose," she said finally. "The word is from my father. Don't ask me any more. We can't talk here. They're only keeping him alive until they get his papers."

"That's interesting," I said. "Why don't you tell the truth?"

She raised her hands helplessly. "It is the truth — it is, if you only understood the situation." She rose. "This is too dangerous. I must be going now. They are listening at the door. Won't you trust me? Won't you believe me? They're going to kill you. I swear they are. You're caught in something that's desperate. They would have killed you already if it weren't for that American friend of yours—that Mr. Bloom on this ship. They don't want him to suspect anything. You'll be safe until he leaves at Shanghai tomorrow. Casey, will you listen to me, please? When this ship comes into the river opposite the city, as it will early tomorrow morning, open that porthole, jump out and swim ashore. Throw the crank out when you go, or they'll know I brought it to you. If you have trouble, ask for a man named Wu Lai-fu and tell him what has happened. Say the name to anyone along the shore, and then go away and never come back! Ask Wu Lai-fu to help you. He's the only one who will. I sha'n't see you again, I think. Good-by—" She looked younger when she said it. Her eyes were begging me to believe her. She looked unhappy—close to tears.

"Thanks for that window crank," I whispered. "I'll throw it out."

"And one thing more," her voice was strained.

"Don't eat anything they give you, Casey Lee. Hide some of it, as though you had. Don't touch anything — do you hear?"

"Thanks," I answered. Now that she was leaving, I was grateful and I wanted to show her that I was grateful. I took her hand, a small cold hand. "You weren't meant for this, Sonya," I said.

"No," she answered. "Neither were you. God help you, Casey Lee."

I wanted to speak to her again, but she shook her head and opened the door. I heard it locked behind her, but she still seemed to be there in the cabin. There was a suspicion of that gardenia perfume and the window crank was in my hand. . . . Who was she? I did not know. What was she? I did not know. But at last I was sure that she had meant kindly by me, that she had risked more than I cared to consider by telling me what she had. What did she mean by her allusion to her father and his papers? It was more than I could tell. Nevertheless, it added to the sum of knowledge in my possession to an extent that made me aware that somehow my country was involved, and this suspicion made me stubborn. The dead man Ma had asked me to communicate with Jim Driscoll and I was determined to do it, if I lived.

There is no need to describe the day of waiting, shut in that cabin, or the night either. The steward brought my luncheon in and I tucked part of it away in my suitcase as Sonya had suggested. At seven in the evening there was another tap on the door, and in came dinner with a bottle of champagne. A visiting card was tied around the bottle, bearing Mr. Moto's name and four words were scrawled beneath it. "With my sincerest compliments." I left the bottle untouched, but stored away some more of the food. No one came to take the tray away. I was not disturbed again. They may have had their reasons for believing that I could make no trouble after the evening meal. I lay for a long while on my bed, listening to the noise of the ship. I must have dozed off in spite of myself, for my next recollection was one of smoothness, and my cabin window was dusky with early dawn. I stared out for a while upon a strange world that was different from Japan, teeming with a patient vitality, serene, in spite of poverty, famine and war — the world of China. The ship was running at half speed up a broad river called the Whangpoo, as I found out later, one of those tributaries on the watery delta of the great Yellow River, connecting the city of Shanghai with the sea. The water flowing past our ship was colored a thick sedimentary yellow which reminded me of the muddy rivulets one made in the country as a child, when the frost has left the ground in spring. The current, I saw, was swift and the distance from shore was wide enough to make me doubt my ability to swim it. The shore itself was low, with green fields which I learned later were rice fields squared off by dykes and ditches. The life on the river was amazing to a stranger who had never seen the East. Besides occasional launches and tugs which might have plied a waterway at home, there were Chinese junks under sail, moving ponderously under great banks of brown canvas slatted with bamboo, looking like an illustration from a book — the relics of another age. They seemed to be as high in the bow and poop as the vessels of Columbus, and at the bow of each a pair of painted eyes made the hulls look like living monsters. Aboard one of them that passed near us a crew stripped to the waist was pulling her mainsail halyard, singing a rhythmic chanty that might have risen from the capstan of a clipper ship. I wished I might have been with them there aboard that junk. Then, in addition to these sailing vessels, the river was filled with smaller craft which were propelled by men with huge sculling oars, and which had deckhouses of matting in their bows. Now and then one of these boats moved hopefully toward the *Imoto Maru,* and once I saw the owner picking up refuse with a net. I only knew later that I was having a glimpse of a strange side of Chinese life — the river life of China, and of a river fleet on which men lived and died without hardly ever stepping onto land. But that first glance gave the impression of a land so teeming with humanity that part of that humanity was pushed into the water.

Even in that gray of early morning I could tell that we were coming to a country where life was cheap because of its abundance. A short time later I saw buildings and wharfs along the shore. From the size of the place, this could be nothing but Shanghai and if Sonya was right, it was time for me to go, provided I wished to live.

I made my preparations quickly, since they were

completely simple. First I shot the bolt on my door, then I kicked off my shoes, took off my coat, and wrapped my scanty supply of money with my passport inside my oilskin tobacco pouch. As I did so, my glance fell on my flask and I jammed it into my hip pocket also, in the belief that I might need a drink if I should be cold and tired. Then, as quietly as I could, I began opening the port. Something — I have never known what — must have made some watcher outside my door suspicious, for just as the window was halfway down, I heard the doorknob turn and then there was a knocking. I did not answer that knock. No cabin window ever went down as fast as mine, and a moment later I had wriggled my shoulders through it and stared into a surge of yellow water. There was no chance to dive. A straight fall of easily twenty feet out of the ship was all that I could achieve. Even that fall was not too soon, for when I was in mid-air I heard a shout which warned me that someone had seen me go. I struck the water flat with a force that shook me badly, without shaking my sense entirely away. Once under water, I stayed until my lungs were nearly bursting. Then, when I came to the surface for breath, I had a glimpse of the ship behind me. They had seen me. I heard shouts and saw men leaning over the rail. Someone had whipped out a pistol and I dived for a second time. When I rose again, the force of the current had driven me away from the ship — perhaps for a hundred yards. I was gasping for breath and struggling with that current when I saw one of those small boats beside me. Just as I saw it, I knew that I would never have the strength to reach the shore, so I struck out toward it and snatched upward at its side. Then a wiry muscular arm reached out and seized my collar, and then another arm. I found myself being lifted bodily out of the water, choking.

There was an excited chattering of voices around me. Shrieks of children, squawks of chickens, and a grunting of pigs. I was on one of those vessels which I had seen following the ship, lying on my back in a cargo space, looking forward at the entrance of a matting-covered cabin. I was surprised at the number of persons on that small craft. There must have been three generations, all family, there, staring at me. An old man with a drooping wisp of gray mustache, bare to the waist, with ragged trousers, was asking me some question. Women were staring at me from under the matting cabin. Three younger men had dropped the sculling oar and were shouting excitedly at their elder; and children, boys and girls in ragged cotton clothes, round-faced, with dark slits of eyes, seemed to be crawling from every crack. The old man was pointing over the side, shouting at me, and I could gather what he meant by his gestures. He was preparing to take me back to the *Imoto Maru*. I shook my head.

"No, no!" I shouted, but it did no good. And then I remembered the name — the name which both Ma and Sonya had mentioned. I pulled myself up to a sitting posture, choking a cough.

"No, no!" I shouted at them. "Wu Lai-fu!"

I have never known three syllables to have such a definite result. The old man looked startled. The younger ones stopped their talking, and taking advantage of the pause, I reached in my hip pocket and drew out a handful of money and pointed to the land.

"Wu Lai-fu," I said again.

No masonic symbol could have been more useful. The old man bowed and took the money. The younger ones leaped to the sculling oar and began working toward the shore. I staggered to my feet and looked across the water at the black hull of the *Imoto Maru*. They had seen what had happened; an officer on her bridge was shouting at us through a megaphone, and to my surprise the crew was lowering a boat. I cupped my hands and shouted over the water.

"Good-by, Mr. Moto," I shouted. "Excuse me, please. I am so very, very sorry."

CHAPTER VIII

No remark I had made in a long while seemed to me so laden with wit or gave me greater pleasure. It was so scintillating from my own viewpoint that I began to laugh, and to my surprise, that boatload of strangers began to laugh too, either out of politeness, or because they had some intuitive idea of what was happening. At any rate, their interest in working in toward shore was most intense and gratifying. The men at the scull were bending at their work, grunting sharply as their bodies moved back and forth, while the old man stood beside me, staring at the ship. Finally he nudged me with his elbow, pointed and displayed a row of toothless gums. The lifeboat was being raised again; with good reason, I think, for we were in the middle of other small craft by then, all of such conventional pattern that it would have been hard to have picked us from the rest. Then the reaction came over me and my teeth began to chatter, but in spite of my physical wretchedness, I shall never forget the sights of that early morning, because they were as unfamiliar to me as though I had arrived upon the moon. The boat was being worked into a bay or inlet below a great modern city whose tall buildings were rising out of the morning mist. The body of water was jammed so thickly with boats and small craft that one could walk to shore by stepping from boat to boat, for almost half a mile, so that the cove had been transformed into a floating city, where every craft seemed to have a definite place. The laundry was hanging out to dry and women were scolding and food was cooking and babies were squealing wherever one cared to look. Our boat ran up alongside some others near the shore and our men made it fast. Then one of the young men started to go ashore and I had leisure to look at the people about me. We all had an excellent chance to examine each other, due to an almost complete lack of privacy and inhibition. The crews from the other junks and their women and children began to gather around us until, as I stood there in the hold, I seemed to be in an amphitheater, surrounded by curious chattering people, yet I always remember they were friendly enough and even merry. One of the old women, who handed me a cup of tea, motioned me inside the matting cabin to sit down. Tea never tasted better than the cup I drank there, enthroned on a pile of rags which were probably filthy with vermin; but I was in no condition to worry about cleanliness. The old man was repeating "Wu Lai-fu" and motioning me to be patient.

I can still see that crowd in my imagination gathered about me in a gradually contracting semicircle, staring. Whenever my mind brings back their faces and rags, an impression of China comes with them which has never been erased. Paradoxically, perhaps, in spite of their stark poverty and evidences of disease and of grinding labor, that impression has always been one of peace. It was a peace born of a knowledge of life and of human relationships. I could understand why China had absorbed her conquerors when I watched that ring of faces. Their bland patience was impervious to any fortune. They stood there staring at me, speaking softly, laughing now and then. . . .

There I was, soaking wet, without other clothes, almost without money, waiting for something or nothing. Now that I come to think of it, I did not have so long to wait, three quarters of an hour perhaps, before there was a stir in the crowd around me and a young man in a long gray Chinese gown, wearing a European felt hat, stepped over the side of the boat.

"You wish to see Wu Lai-fu?" he asked. His face was lean and intelligent; he spoke in very good English, with an enunciation better than my own. He did not seem in the least surprised to see me sitting there, dripping wet out of the river.

"Who told you," he asked, "to see Wu Lai-fu?"

"A Chinese named Ma," I said, "on the Japanese boat. They killed him."

He betrayed no surprise, if he felt any, but my explanation must have satisfied him. He waved a hand toward me, a thin hand that emerged gracefully from the loose gray sleeve of his gown.

"You come with me," he said, and that was all. We walked from boat to boat until we reached the shore, without any further explanation.

Once we were ashore there were two other Chinese waiting for us, dressed, like my companion, in long gray gowns. One of them moved to one side of me and the other walked behind us.

"It is all right," the first man said. "Do not be alarmed. We will take you in an automobile. Here it is."

My next memory was being shown into the interior of a large American limousine, where I was placed between two Chinese and was looking at the backs of two others in the driver's seat. The swiftness of the whole procedure struck me as disturbing. Although the car was parked in a narrow street of shops with Chinese signs, something in the appearance of my companions gave me an impression of the Chicago underworld — and a suspicion that I was going for a ride. No American chauffeur ever drove faster or more recklessly than that Chinese driver. We were off a second later with our horn blowing steadily, twisting through a labyrinth of streets which might have been in the moon, for anything I could tell. The man beside me spoke again, politely:

"You know Shanghai?"

"No," I said.

"You know China?"

"No," I said.

"Shanghai is a very nice city," he remarked.

As though directly to contradict his statement, something went slap against the window of the limousine with a sound that made me duck my head. The men on either side of me looked interested but not disturbed.

"Do not be afraid," my companion said. "The glass is bullet-proof. Someone, I think, does not like you very much."

We must have ridden for fifteen minutes, perhaps longer, through very crowded streets, when the car drew up before an unprepossessing gate in a high gray wall. They must have been expecting us because the gate opened at the sound of the motor horn and six or seven large-boned, slant-eyed men stepped out and gazed searchingly up and down.

"What's the matter?" I asked. "Is there going to be a war?"

My sallow-faced companion smiled slightly. "There is always something of a war. Come, please. Walk quickly in!" A second later we were in a courtyard with low tile-roofed buildings about it that gave one the idea of an entrance to a prison. The Chinese who were standing there had a semi-official, military manner; all of them were large men, impressively so, after my experiences in Japan.

"What is this place?" I asked.

"You are coming to the home of Wu Lai-fu," my guide answered. "Will you please to step this way?" We walked across the court into a smaller one and then along a covered gallery into a building on the right.

I was surprised, when we were inside the building, to find that the interior was comfortable according to foreign standards. We were in a bedroom with teakwood chairs and scroll pictures on the wall, where two men in white gowns, evidently servants, were waiting. My guide spoke to them rapidly.

"You are to bathe and change your clothes," he said. "There is a hot bath running for you and they will bring you eggs and fruit and coffee. We have only Chinese clothes. You do not mind?"

I was too confused to be surprised or to thank him. All these impressions, which had come so suddenly upon me, have made my recollections of the entrance into that place vague, and nothing seemed to me strange by then, not the pillars in the court-yards or curving tiled roofs or marble dragons by the gates. I only recollect that no English valets could have waited on me more conscientiously or correctly than those men. They helped me into a tiled bathroom and into a tub of steaming hot water. Next I was in a silk suit of pajamas, with a robe buttoned over it, eating an excellent breakfast with a knife and fork. I ate in a sort of daze and went through all the motions of dressing without asking any questions, while the servants stood at-tentively by me. I had just finished my coffee and one of them had offered me a cigarette from a silver box when my guide returned.

"Wu Lai-fu will see you now," he said.

I have no coherent idea of the establishment of Wu Lai-fu, but only the recollection of walking through buildings and through courtyards until we came to a large room which was part Oriental and part European. A blue carpet with yellow dragons was on the floor. The furniture was black lacquer. There were two paintings on silk of old landscapes on the wall, and a large commercial map of China. At the end of the room there was an office desk with two telephones upon it, and a typewriter stood upon the table beside it. A middle-aged man sat behind the desk, with his hands folded in front of him, a Chinese in a plain black robe. His closely shaved head was partly gray and his face had an ageless, reposed expression, as though all emotion had evaporated. The man might have been forty or sixty — a slim man who looked at me through a pair of horn-rimmed spectacles like a school-teacher or a scholar. He nodded to my guide, who left the room at his nod, closing the door and leaving me standing before the desk. This man was not like Mr. Moto. He showed no anxiety or nervousness, but only a placid calmness.

"I am Wu Lai-fu," the man behind the desk said. "What is your name, please?"

"My name is K. C. Lee," I answered.

He did not answer for a moment, but sat with his hands clasped on the desk.

"I suppose," he said — his English was flawless — "you do not know who I am?"

"No," I answered.

He smiled, and his whole face broke into arid wrinkles. "Then I will tell you," he said. "Your countrymen say I am the wickedest man in China. They say I control various guilds in this city, including the thieves and prostitutes. As a matter of fact, I am a merchant, whose business has connections. I hope you will tell me the truth, because if I have the slightest doubt that you do not — and I understand the faces of you foreigners — if I find that you are lying, I can make you tell the truth."

His manner was contemptuous, as though he were speaking to a barbarian; it was the first time that I had the feeling that I was a savage. I can never explain, but in some way I had the sense that his race was vastly older than mine and older even than Mr. Moto's. I could believe that the thin ascetic man in his black robe was living in another world of intellect.

"Are you threatening me, Mr. Wu?" I asked.

"Exactly," the other said. "I am asking you to tell the truth. Tell it quickly, please."

"You have the advantage of me, Mr. Wu," I said.

His hands on the desk moved, but his face did not.

"Yes," he answered. "So much so that it is my pleasure to be frank. Some day I hope to see you and all of your kind driven into the sea."

I felt my face growing red. "No one asked me here," I answered. "I came here as a stranger. I have always heard of your courtesy, but now I know that you have bad manners."

Mr. Wu shook his head but he did not smile. "It seems to me you've been treated with courtesy," he said. "You were picked out of the river like a half-drowned rat. You were brought to my house. You were bathed and fed. You are standing before me in my clothes. The lowest Chinese coolie would have bowed to me and thanked me. You have not thanked me, Mr. Lee. What do you know of manners?"

"I know enough," I said, "not to threaten a guest beneath my roof. If I picked you up like a rat, Mr. Wu, I should have treated you better."

"Ah, but you have not a roof," he answered. "You have nothing. What is the English phrase? You must sing for your supper, Mr. Lee. Please sing, because I am busy. Why did you jump off a comfortable steamer into our Wangpoo River?"

"Because they were going to murder me," I said.

"Who were?" he asked.

"A Japanese named Moto," I answered.

The thin hands on the desk closed together tighter, but Mr. Wu's composure was not altered. "Why?" he asked.

"They thought I had a message from one of your countrymen," I said. "His name was Ma, and that's all I know about it, Mr. Wu."

Mr. Wu sat for a moment, watching me coolly. "Where is Ma?" he asked.

"Dead," I answered. "They killed him in my cabin."

Mr. Wu's lips moved but everything else about him was motionless. "There are many Chinese lives," he said. "Where is the message? I wish you to tell me promptly — and truthfully — or I shall call on men who can make you."

I looked at the dragons on the carpet. The dragons seemed to be writhing toward me slowly, as it came over me that Mr. Wu wanted the message too, as poignantly as Mr. Moto wanted it. I wondered if he would believe me. I hoped he would, because he was not bluffing.

"Mr. Wu," I answered, "I have not got that message."

"Ah," said Mr. Wu; "they found it then?"

"No," I answered, "they did not find it. They thought I had read it and destroyed it."

Mr. Wu unclasped his hands and tapped a bell beside the desk, and then the thing that happened has always been hard to believe. I had to tell myself that I was Casey Lee, and yet I might have been in the Middle Ages that next moment. A door opened behind me at the sound of that bell and four men walked through it. Two of them seized my arms, while two others stood beside them, holding ropes and wooden and iron instruments.

"And now," said Mr. Wu, "you will tell me what the message is — sooner or later."

I tried to keep my voice steady. "I told you," I answered, "I have never seen that message." And then I had another thought. "Before Ma died — the night before — he spoke to me. He told me to deliver that message if he should give it to me, to a commander in our navy. If I had it, he should have it — not you, Mr. Wu. And if I knew that message, which

150

I don't, you could cut me to pieces before I said a word."

"I wonder," said Mr. Wu softly, "I wonder — "

"You needn't wonder," I answered. "Go ahead and try!"

"You are brave," said Mr. Wu softly. "Savages are always brave." Then he spoke to the men and they dropped my arms. "I think you had better tell me everything, Mr. Lee — everything from the beginning." He spoke again and one of the men moved up a chair. I dropped into it, because my knees were weak.

"I will if you give me a drink," I said.

"Drink — " Mr. Wu smiled slightly. "So you have a drunkard's courage? Very well, you shall have your drink."

I gripped the arms of the lacquer chair. That taunt of Mr. Wu's stung more than the remark of any prohibitionist. "Never mind the drink then," I said. "I don't need it to talk to you! Furthermore, I've been in worse spots than this. I'm not afraid."

Mr. Wu smiled again. "Oh, yes," he said; "oh, yes, you are. . . ." He was speaking the truth and he knew I knew it.

"Perhaps," i said, "I am, but it doesn't make any difference, because I haven't anything to tell you."

Mr. Wu leaned back in his chair and folded his arms in his sleeves. "Now," he said, "you're speaking the truth, and that's what I want — the truth, and nothing more. And then we will have no trouble, Mr. Lee."

"As a matter of fact, I should rather like to know the truth myself," I said. "I don't understand what's happened, Mr. Wu."

Mr. Wu smiled again. "And you probably never will know," he answered. "Why should you? I am not depending upon your rather turgid intellect. Who paid you to come here?"

"A Japanese," I answered, "named Moto."

"Ah," said Mr. Wu, "so you've been hired by them, have you?"

The unbiased accuracy of his words made me more keenly aware of what I had done than I had ever been before. "I'm not proud of it," I explained. "I rather think that's over, since Mr. Moto tried to murder me."

Mr. Wu leaned further forward across the desk. "I think you'd better tell me the circumstances," he said softly. "How did you meet this countryman of mine named Ma? And what was it that Mr. Moto wanted you to do?"

I could never in my life have believed that anyone like Mr. Wu existed, but he was completely believable then. Although I disliked him, I found myself telling him frankly, with hardly a reservation, what had happened. I told him about the visitor in my stateroom. I quoted our conversation word for word, while Mr. Wu sat there listening to me, never moving a muscle of his face or hands.

"So you were in the American navy," he remarked, "and an aviator. We are interested in aviation here. It is one hope for a weak, disorganized nation. You are not, by any chance, interested in naval design, Mr. Lee?"

"No," I said, "not in the least."

"You have never been a naval architect?" Mr. Wu asked softly. "Or studied fuel combustion?"

"No," I said.

Although he did not move, I could see that he was taking all my words, weighing them, polishing them in his mind and working them into a pattern. "That is very curious," he said. "There was a message. Now there is no message. Ma was a very capable man. He had a sense of habit and behavior. I have dealt with Ma."

I sat in front of the desk, and the room was very still while I looked curiously at the man who sat there thinking.

"You spoke of a Russian," he said finally. "A woman or a girl? Tell me what she looks like, that is, if you possess sufficient powers of observation."

I described Sonya to him as carefully as I could and for the first time his placidity left him. His eyes sharpened and he rubbed his hands together.

"So she was there," he said, "and she found nothing, also. That is interesting, Mr. Lee." He tapped the bell on his desk again. I am free to confess that the sound sent a shiver down my spine, but only a servant entered at the signal. Mr. Wu spoke to him in his elusive language, evidently a question, and then he smiled at me when he got his answer. His entire manner changed with his smile. There was no cruelty left in him, but instead, the sympathy and anxiety of a host.

"I am asking the man to bring me whisky," he

said. "And I beg of you to take it. The trouble is over now. Sit down, Mr. Lee, and be as comfortable as you can in your strange clothes. Some others have been ordered for you already — the impractical useless garments of the foreigners, if you will excuse my saying so. I am intensely nationalistic, Mr. Lee; intensely racial might be a better expression. I am proud of my own people and I have seen many of them. They are superior to other people. Do not disturb yourself. The trouble is over now — because I have found you have told the truth."

"What are you going to do with me?" I asked.

Mr. Wu raised his thin hand. "I do not blame you," he remarked, "for being worried about yourself. Your face tells me that you have thought only of self for many, many years. There is nothing in this world more unfortunate. What am I going to do with you? You must wait and see." Just as he finished speaking, the servant came back, stepping noiselessly across the heavy carpet. The servant said something and Mr. Wu rubbed his hands again. His expression had become almost benign and kind when the servant had finished speaking.

"Do not speak, please, Mr. Lee," he said. "You

must excuse me. I have important matters on my mind. I congratulate you that you have told the truth. This girl you speak of — I wish that she were here."

I thanked heaven that Sonya was not there. "She doesn't know anything," I said.

"Perhaps I can find out." Mr. Wu's voice was calm. He had picked up one of his telephones and was evidently calling for some number. He listened attentively, then he spoke in a singsong cadence, set down the instrument and rang the bell and gave another order to the servant.

"I will not keep you much longer, Mr. Lee," he said; "only a moment, please." His dark narrow eyes were intent, but, as he continued speaking, I think his mind was somewhere else and he was only speaking to pass the time. "You do not know China? It is a sad country," he said; "the most exploited country in the world. The barbarians are snatching at her again. The Japanese are barbarians and the Russians — But we may perfect our own methods some day."

"If the Chinese are all like you, I am sure they will," I said.

"Thank you," said Mr. Wu. "Unfortunately, they are not all like me."

I heard the door open behind me and then I heard a voice which made me start — the throaty voice of the Russian girl named Sonya. There she was, walking across the dragon carpet, in white with her sables around her shoulders, a white suède bag clasped under her arm. I felt those violet eyes of hers upon me for a moment in a cool guileless glance.

"So he came here safely," she said.

"Yes," said Mr. Wu, "you did very well to send him here."

I found my voice with difficulty.

"Sonya — " I began.

"This was better for you than being killed, Casey," she said simply.

My voice grew sharper as I answered. "Where do you fit into this picture, Sonya?"

"Does it make any difference?" she asked me, and there was a mockery in the way she spoke. "Haven't you had nearly enough trouble?"

Mr. Wu was smiling. He was standing up straight behind his desk, his hands folded beneath his sleeves.

"Yes," he said, "I think you have had enough, Mr.

Lee, and I am obliged to you. Your clothing will be waiting for you and a sum of money for your pocket. You will be taken to your foreign quarter, where no doubt you can go and drink yourself into a stupor. If you do not move out of it, except to take the first boat to your native land, perhaps you will be safe. Good-by, Mr. Lee."

"Sonya—" I said again. I tried to frame some question but hesitated and stopped.

"Yes, Casey," she said, "now that this is over, I think you had better take the next boat home. You were not meant for this. It is not your fault."

Even then it amazed me that in my position I should feel angry and hurt. It seemed to me that Sonya's manner had something of the superciliousness of Mr. Wu's. The door had opened and a white-robed servant was standing in the doorway.

"Sonya," I said—I spoke to her instead of to Wu—"you think I'm a fool, don't you? I don't understand a single thing that's happening here but I don't like it. You're not finished with me yet."

Mr. Wu nodded as though my speech had confirmed some thought in his own mind.

"Foreigners always boast," he said. "Foreigners

always grow angry. You have no idea how much you are to be congratulated, Mr. Lee, that you are leaving here in such a pleasant manner. Now I advise you to leave at once before you are made to leave more quickly."

I looked at Sonya again. "Good-by," I said.

I walked out of the doorway with the man in white at my elbow, assiduous and polite. I was so much disturbed by the whole affair that I paid no attention to where we were going. I felt a deep humiliation at everything which had happened. The thinly veiled sarcasm of Mr. Wu had not been lost upon me. He thought that I was an irresponsible drunkard, who had been tossed up by the sea. There had been a moment — I could not tell just when — in which his interest in me had suddenly vanished. Something inexplicable had happened which had made me as useless to him as a sucked orange. He had extracted something from me without my being able to tell what. He had been anxious about that message to the point of trying to extort it and then his anxiety had waned. It had waned before Sonya had appeared seemingly out of nowhere.

That whole scene and that whole place has always

been to me like a page of an Oriental romance, with no bearing on the actual life I have known. Perhaps the Orient is all like that. There may be in every Oriental a love of involved dramatics and fantasy that is expressed to us by the pages of the "Arabian Nights." I do not know about this and I do not care, because I am only trying to state the actual facts as they occurred.

Once I was back in the room where I had been dressed, I had a proof of Mr. Wu's prosperity. A new and very good European suit, with shoes and linen, was waiting for me, and even a suitcase with a change of clothing. One of the servants explained the appearance of these articles in English, the first time I knew that he was familiar with the language.

"You take," he said, "compliments of Mr. Wu. Mr. Wu he say the motor wagon waits for you."

Fifteen minutes later I found myself dressed in a gray flannel suit which did not fit me badly. One of the men was handing me a gray felt hat and a cane, the other had lifted my bag and I had turned to leave the room, when one of the servants spoke.

"Please," he said, "the master has forgotten. His money and his flask." And he handed me my tobacco pouch, containing my Japanese notes and my passport and my leather-covered flask with the metal cup in place at the bottom. I was glad to have my flask, for it seemed like an old friend, the only link that connected me with a previous incarnation — a doubtful one perhaps, but one in which I possessed my own integrity.

I set my hat on the back of my head and tossed a ten-yen note to the servants.

"All right, boys," I said, "let's go!"

Then there was a walk through that labyrinth of courtyards and I was out of the gate where that same motor which had conveyed me there was waiting. I was inside it with my bag and the gate had closed behind me. The car started with no directions of mine, evidently because the driver had already received his orders. While I leaned back in the seat, without interest in the sights I saw, absorbed in my own thoughts, for the first time in many years I was thinking consecutively and fast; not of myself, for the first time in years, but of something more important than myself. If Driscoll were in this city, and I recalled that he had spoken of coming here, I knew that I must find him. Something was going on of actual importance. Men did not act as Moto and Wu Lai-fu had acted without grave cause. I did not have the message, but I had sense enough to know that there might be significant details in my adventure which a man in Driscoll's position could understand. Clearly, in some way beyond my knowledge, the interests of my country were at stake. It seemed strange to me that I must see Driscoll.

I had another impression besides these thoughts which I have not forgotten; that impression came upon me suddenly with the motion of the motor car, without the interposition of any specific sight or sound. I was aware that I was in a strange place where anything might happen, and believe me, I was right. I doubt if any city in the world is more amazing than Shanghai, where the culture of the East and West has met to turn curiously into something different than East and West; where the silver and riches of China are hoarded for safety; where *opéra-bouffe* Oriental millionaires drive their limousines along the Bund; where the interests of Europe meet the Orient and clash in a sparkle of uniforms and jewels; where the practical realities of Western industrialism meet the fatality of the East. I say I could feel this thing, and now I only state it as an explanation of Mr. Wu and of the events which follow. Believe me, I repeat, anything can happen in Shanghai, from a sordid European intrigue to a meeting with a prince.

CHAPTER IX

THE automobile took me out of China into a city which might have been planted there from Europe or America, except for the rickshaw boys and the Chinese faces on the street. There were skyscrapers and stone buildings with all the tradition of the Renaissance, which looked upon warships from Europe and liners and junks floating on the muddy yellow waters of the Whangpoo. I could feel an excitement in the air, as though history were in the making, as though I were present at the changing of a world, and I have never forgotten that excitement. The car stopped at the door of an excellent hotel, where a doorman in livery took my bags. At the sight of my own people, seated drinking at little tables in the lounge, at the sight of its calm and order (I remembered that there was even a notice of the meeting of the Rotary Club posted in white letters on a bulletin board), I felt the security of things I knew. Once again I could almost believe that everything which had happened to me had been a dream. As I walked up to the hotel desk, I could hardly conceive that I was the man who had jumped through the port of a vessel to avoid death, or the man who had been picked up like a drowned rat, as Mr. Wu had said, from the waters of the Whangpoo. The clerk at the desk was handing me a registry card, after the custom of the best hotels at home.

"Can you tell me," I asked him, "where I can find a naval officer named Commander Driscoll?" In the light of everything which I had gone through, the casualness of his answer did not seem logical.

"Certainly, sir," he answered. "Commander Driscoll is staying at this hotel — Room 507. Do you wish to see him, sir?" He reached toward a telephone. "May I ask the name?"

"Tell him Lee," I answered. "K. C. Lee, and have my bag sent to my room." I heard him speak into the telephone. The Chinese boy in the smart uniform of a bellhop bowed to me and pointed to a lift. I had not recovered from the unreality of returning to my own world before we were standing before a room door where the clerk had told me Driscoll lived. I knocked and the door opened. The door opened and seemed to admit me back again to my own people, for there was Jim Driscoll, heavy and stocky, standing on the threshold staring at me, and as I glanced across his shoulder, I saw May Driscoll, Jim's wife. It seemed a thousand years ago, before the fall of Babylon, that I had known such people.

"How did you get here?" Jim Driscoll asked. "And what do you want here?" His manner was neither friendly nor approving. He was no longer looking at me as a friend or as a member of his own caste, but as an unsavory stranger.

"Jim," I said, "I want to talk to you. Something important, or I wouldn't be here now."

Driscoll turned toward his wife. "May," he said, "you'd better go into the bedroom and close the door."

I heard May laugh. "Why, Jim," she said, "it's Casey. Hello, Casey darling — Can't I talk to Casey, Jim?"

"No," Jim Driscoll said. "You heard me, May. Please go in there and close the door." And Jim Driscoll and I stood facing each other in the parlor of a hotel suite decorated with all the curious lack of taste which is common to any hotel suite.

"All right," Jim Driscoll said; "what do you want? Are you drunk or sober, Lee?"

"Sober, Jim," I said. "Cold sober."

He laughed shortly. "Are you? With a flask sticking out of your pocket?"

"That doesn't mean —" I began.

"Doesn't it?" Jim Driscoll inquired. "Not that it makes any difference, after Tokio."

I tried to keep my temper. "I want to tell you something," I said. "Are you in the Naval Intelligence?"

He nodded shortly. "All right," I continued, "a Chinese told me to give you a message. His name was Ma. He was murdered on the *Imoto Maru.*"

As I was speaking, Driscoll had been pacing in front of me, a habit which he probably acquired from shipboard; but at the name of Ma he stopped dead in his tracks. He stopped and spun on his heel and puckered up his eyes.

"Ma," he said, as though I were not there. "That's old Karaloff's man!" He closed his hands and opened them and took a step toward me. "Where did you pick up this bit?" he inquired. "Are you serious?"

"Yes," I said. "I'm telling you the sober truth. I ought to know, because that man Ma was murdered in my cabin on the *Imoto Maru*."

Jim Driscoll snorted contemptuously. "The sober truth," he said. "It's been quite a while since you told that. How did you get on the *Imoto Maru*? The last time I saw you, you were pickled in Tokio. What got you aboard that ship?"

It was difficult for me to remember that I had come with information that was more important than my own feelings, because Driscoll's manner was not conciliating, and I have never been good at restraining my temper.

"Jim," I said, "I'm taking this from you because this may be more important than you or I. You remember there in the hotel, the way I was talking? Well, someone heard me. A man named Moto."

Jim Driscoll swore. "So that's the play, is it?" he said. "And what did this man Moto look like?"

"What do any Japanese look like?" I inquired. "He was small, almost delicate. He wore a morning coat, little feet, little hands — intelligent, polite. He could speak English as well as you can. Patent-leather shoes, a green ring on his finger. He kept saying he was so very, very sorry."

Jim Driscoll exhaled a deep breath and moved a step nearer to me. I might have been a prisoner being interrogated by the military police.

"By God," said Driscoll, "that's the baby! Lee, what is your relationship with that man? How did he get hold of you?"

"He offered to supply a plane so that I could fly across the Pacific," I answered, "for certain considerations. My tobacco company welched on me. There I was."

Jim Driscoll turned his back on me, paced across the room and back. "You might be a little steadier if you had a drink," he suggested. "Eh, what, Lee? Your mind might move along a more even groove. It probably takes a drink to give you guts. All right —" He opened a closet door and pulled out a bottle of Scotch and a glass.

"Thanks," I said. "Are you joining me?"

Jim Driscoll snorted through his nose. "It isn't my business to drink with everyone," he said. "I'm giving you a drink for medicinal reasons, Lee. Help yourself."

I pushed away the bottle. "When I'm through here," I said, "I promise you I won't trouble you again."

Jim Driscoll laughed. "That's mutual," he answered. "And now, so we can reach that point, perhaps you'll tell me exactly what happened to you."

I told him; for the second time that night, I told the truth. And as I did so, I could not help comparing Driscoll unfavorably with the black-robed Wu Lai-fu. Against that other man Driscoll seemed blunt and stupid and incapable of any act of brilliance. Although he listened to me carefully, I wondered if he caught any real significance in what I said. I did not believe that anything much registered with him, to judge from the opinion which he rendered after he listened to me. He paced up and down the room again and halted in front of me.

"There's one thing obvious," he remarked; "you can't be trusted."

I felt my self-control leaving me. "That is hardly fair," I said.

Driscoll smiled with an elephantine sort of politeness. "Please excuse me," he answered. "I didn't mean to hurt your feelings. Have you got any feelings left, Lee? I gather you're a spy in the pay of Japan. You can't blame me for wondering exactly what your position is. So you haven't got the message? Is that all you came to tell me?"

"I thought maybe you could do something," I answered. "But, of course, I was mistaken in that. You always were a dumbbell, Jim — just one of the routine people who gets ahead in the Service." It pleased me to perceive that my remark nettled him.

"Thanks," he answered, and walked to the room telephone, and called out a number in the same way he might have signalled the engine room from the bridge. "So Wu Lai-fu's in it, is he? You've got yourself into pretty company. All right, I want to see Wu — " His voice trailed off and changed into Chinese, as someone answered from the other end of the wire, reminding me that Driscoll had been a language officer in Peking. He talked for nearly a minute, unintelligibly, finally turning to me again when he had finished.

"We'll get this straightened out here and now," he said. "Wu's coming here himself. There must be something in the air to make that fellow call. This is serious and we've got to get on with it. . . . Now this Russian girl—what did you say her name was?"

"You heard me," I answered. "Sonya."

Driscoll gazed at me pityingly. "Who in hell cares about first names?" he inquired. "Are you sure you don't need a drink to pull your wits together? Use your mind. What was her last name?"

I tried to think, but my indignation made thinking difficult. "I'm trying to think," I replied. "She told me once—yes, I've got it now—she told me her last name was Karaloff."

Driscoll's manner changed. His mouth dropped open and he stood stock-still. Whatever the name might have meant to him, I knew it was important.

"That tears it," he said softly, seemingly to himself. "It doesn't seem possible, but I believe it's right," and he began to grin. "Lee, you've earned a drink. By God, that will be Karaloff's daughter! That's important! Help yourself! There's the bottle, Lee."

I pushed the bottle away. "Not your whisky," I said. "Who's the old man?"

Driscoll laughed again. "If you don't know, it won't hurt you," he answered. "I'd sooner tell a secret to a microphone than talk to you. But listen, Lee, I want to ask you a favor."

"Can you advance any reason why I should do you a favor under the circumstances?" I asked him.

Driscoll answered earnestly. "Not for me," he said. "I'm asking you in behalf of the land where you were born. In the hope that you have a drop of patriotism left. That girl must like you, Casey, if she tried to save your life. If she likes you, that's something we can use." And he began to pace the floor again.

"What?" I asked.

"We want this message," Driscoll said. "It's strange, the agencies which shape events. It just happens that you have blundered into something through the elements of chance. It may interest you to know that a phase of this business may concern the entire balance of power on the Pacific. Or does it interest you to know?"

"Isn't that your occupation?" I inquired. "Isn't that why you get a cut out of our income taxes? Aren't you a public servant?"

Driscoll ignored my remark.

"Casey," he said, "that girl knows something. We

don't know what. We have no real way of reaching her, but you can." He looked toward the closed door of his bedroom, where he had sent his wife. "You have a way with the ladies. They all love aviators. I ought to know. Now listen to me, Lee. A woman is always the weak link in such an affair as this. She can pry the secrets from the diplomat, and the gigolos can get the secrets from the ladies. You get my idea, Casey?"

"No," I said.

Driscoll became patronizingly patient. "Excuse me for being subtle," he apologized. "Let us come down to words of one syllable. Sex appeal, Casey. It's clear the girl likes you. Well, cultivate her acquaintance. Gain her confidence. You know her. There's an easy and elemental way to do it with which you are familiar. And when," Driscoll smiled, "when you've gained her confidence, when she can't bear to exist without you, ask her about her dear old father. Find out what she knows about the message and work fast, Casey." He looked at the bedroom door again. "I know you're a fast worker."

"And then what do you want?" I asked.

"I want you to trot around here and tell me what

you've found. Do you want money for entertainment? I can help you out."

First it had been Moto, then Sonya, then Wu Lai-fu, and now Driscoll, all asking for that message. I still could only half believe what I had heard. I could only half believe that this man was the same Driscoll I had known in the old days. It was not conceivable that he could think me capable of such an action.

"Jim," I said, "you don't mean that, do you?"

Driscoll looked puzzled. "Don't be a damn fool," he said. "I may have ridden you, Casey, but you deserve to be ridden. This is serious, and I want you to believe it is serious. Go out and get that information from that girl!"

I was still incredulous. "Jim," I asked him, "do you honestly think I will?"

But he was in deadly earnest. He reached out a hand and took me by the shoulder.

"We're not talking about honor, Casey," he said. "There's no honor in this business. This isn't Lady Vere de Vere's drawing room. We're dealing with realities and not with any code of chivalry. That belongs in another incarnation, but not in the Intelligence Service; that's a fact which is recognized by everyone in the game. Now, Casey, this business has been worrying us for months. We've heard rumors of it through our own sources of information. We must get this straight, if we can, no matter what it costs, and you look like our one white hope. I'd go to Wu Lai-fu, but he may swing away from me if he knows too much. You've got to get that girl and bring her into camp."

I struggled with my thoughts again and asked him:

"Is that message so important?"

He moved impatiently. "It's damned important, more important than you or me or any neurotic little Russian skirt." He drew a wallet from his pocket and tossed five hundred dollars in Chinese bills on the table. "There you are. That'll pay your expenses. Get going, Don Juan!"

I looked at the money on the table and back to Driscoll, who waited expectantly, his face molded into the familiar lines of service and duty; and that face was like a mirror, because his opinion of me was reflected in his eyes. His expression resembled the revelation which had come over me that night aboard the boat. I knew that I had come on a long rough road, but I had never completely visualized the end of it until then. That he should think me capable of such a combination was what hurt me most; and yet he must have had his reasons; and Driscoll was no fool. He had made his request after observing my appearance and my conduct, obviously thinking that the matter would be simple and that I would willingly agree. I can remember every detail of that tawdry sitting room — the label on the whisky bottle, the empty glass, the cigarette butts in the ash tray, a lace shawl on an untidy sofa, Driscoll's white-visored cap tossed upon the table.

"All right," I said, "I'll try to get your message."

I saw Driscoll smile with artificial heartiness. "That's the boy," he said. And then his expression changed. I moved closer to him and he must have seen something in my face.

"But not that way," I said. "Listen to me, Driscoll. I'm talking to you now. I came here of my own free will to tell you something, and in return you've made a proposal which I do not like. You don't know this girl."

I did not know why I was so angry until I made

that speech. It was not on account of myself, but because of her.

"Wait a minute!" Jim Driscoll's face grew red. "You don't understand this game."

"No," I said, "and I don't want to understand it. You may be an officer, but you're only a gentleman by act of Congress. If that message is in existence, I'm willing to try to get it my own way, and when I get it, Driscoll, you can have it — and to hell with the whole lot of you! I'm not a gigolo — not yet."

Driscoll opened his mouth and closed it. "Don't be a damn fool," he said. "What are you going to do — make a noble speech?"

Then something snapped, and I lost my self-control.

"I'll show you what I'm going to do," I answered. "That girl's worth any ten of you, Driscoll. At any rate, she saved my life, and you can keep your hands off her."

I drew back my own hand almost without consciousness and brought my palm across his face.

It is amazing sometimes how an act like that will clear the air. I had never intended to take such an action; and the thing which impelled me was entirely beyond my own control. Now that it was over, I think that I was more surprised than Jim Driscoll. His lips, by some sort of reflex, drew back in a stupid grin.

"You don't think I'm going to stand here and take that?" he said.

"Have it your own way," I answered. "You got what was coming to you, and you know what to do if you want some more."

Driscoll rubbed his hand across his cheek. It was interesting to see the effort he made to control his anger.

"We can't go on with this here," he said, "and you probably know it. We'll have to wait till this is over, Casey. I told you — you and I don't matter in this business and maybe this will prove it to you."

It did prove it in a way. I even found myself admiring Driscoll for his self-control.

"Just the same," I answered, "what I said goes and you'd better know it."

"You've been damned obvious," said Driscoll.

"I hope so," I answered. It is useless to speculate where this might have led us, since, fortunately perhaps, a tap on the door interrupted us and Driscoll's anger left him.

"That's Wu," he whispered. "Straighten yourself out and snap into it!" And he opened the hall door.

It was Mr. Wu, right enough. He still wore his black silk gown and he was holding a brown felt hat in his hands, bowing humbly.

"The honor is so great that it makes me afraid," he said. "You have summoned me, Commander Driscoll?"

Driscoll nodded. "Do you mind if we don't go through all the courtesies?" he inquired. "And come straight to the point?"

Mr. Wu set his hat down on the table, thrust his hands inside his sleeves and nodded.

"If you do not care for the amenities, we need not have them," he said. "I can be as direct as you. So you've seen this countryman of yours." His eyes moved toward me thoughtfully. "That is very good. It was my belief that he would come here."

"Was it?" said Driscoll. "You are very astute, Mr. Wu."

"Oh, no," said Mr. Wu and shook his head. "It is only that my people are an old people living in a land so crowded that it has made us familiar with personal relationships. I guess that you are bothered about a certain message. This man has naturally told you of it. Do you think it perhaps has to do with the matter we have spoken of?"

Driscoll looked at him earnestly. "I know it has, Wu," he said, "and I know that you can help me if you want. You came to me a while ago to open negotiations, so I hope we are still working together. What do you know about this message?"

Mr. Wu's expression was studiously blank, but there was a sardonic glint in his eye; and then his lips twisted superciliously. "Yes," he said, "it is true that I did come to you, a while ago — but only as an agent. I am sorry that I cannot help you any longer, Commander Driscoll. I have myself to think of, and now I have decided to take the matter into my own hands. There are so many others interested who may pay better. England perhaps, or Russia perhaps."

"Look here," Driscoll's face grew red, "you came around to me."

Mr. Wu's hands moved out of his sleeves, thin placating hands.

"I did," he answered, "but if you have thought that I was exclusively your servant in this, that was a misunderstanding. I find it better to be by myself just now."

For a second time Driscoll seemed to find it difficult to keep his temper. "By God," he said, "you've double-crossed me, Wu!"

Mr. Wu looked amused. "You put it very crudely," he said. "I simply approached you some time ago. I have given you my word about nothing."

Then I began to laugh. Without knowing exactly what was passing, it was clear enough that Mr. Wu had been a match for Jim Driscoll, and in some way he had extracted something from him and then had left him flat.

"I was afraid you wouldn't be any good, Jim," I told him, "and now I know it. Mr. Wu has got you in a hole, hasn't he? Good-by, Jim. You must excuse him, Mr. Wu. He isn't very bright." I clapped on my hat and had started for the door before I had another thought. "I don't know China or the Chinese, Mr. Wu," I added, "but I know one thing that probably works here the same as it does anywhere. You're too pleased with yourself. Even if you are, it never pays to show it." It seemed to me that Mr. Wu's expression grew sharper, and he might have replied if I had given him a chance to answer, but I did not. Instead, I walked into the hall, leaving Mr. Wu and Driscoll to talk as they pleased.

In spite of Mr. Wu's skill at dissembling, I was more sure than ever that there had been a change in him. That change had occurred when I was talking to him at his house. Mr. Wu knew something which none of us knew and he was very much pleased by his knowledge.

CHAPTER X

I WENT and sat awhile in my own hotel room because I wished to be alone and to think. The room, completely European in its furnishings, looked over the tramcars and automobiles and crowds and turbaned policeman of Nanking Road. But all those foreign sights and sounds are blurred in my memory, only forming a hazy disturbing background which simply served to make my thoughts unpleasant. In my heart, I knew that the words I used to Driscoll could not be backed up by any action of mine. On the contrary, everything which Driscoll had said of me was true. What was going to happen to me when my money ran out, I wondered. Now that I had broken with Mr. Moto, there would be no Pacific flight, if he ever really meant it. There was some hope that Sam Bloom might find me something on some flying field, but this hope was vague enough. As far as finding anything about the message, it was entirely beyond me. I knew I was as close to being finished as I had ever been in my life. I knew it better when I went up to the dining room for lunch. It was a large ambitious dining room with snow-white tables and crystal chandeliers and an orchestra.

There was a superficial gaiety in that place which had a feverish quality of unreality. All the Europeans in Shanghai seemed to be gathered at lunch, each trying to forget something — thick-set business men from their offices and banks, a majority with the heavy faces of confirmed drinkers; naval officers and business men's wives and officers' wives, who all probably knew too much about the private lives of everyone else. There was a furtive undercurrent of gossip and intrigue, combined with an exiled loneliness, resulting from a thousand longing thoughts of home. I could believe that no one there was happy, that no one was entirely at ease. At any rate, the atmosphere served to intensify my own restlessness. I was glad to go back to my own room again, in spite of my having no real reason to go there. I had no reason to do anything, and it occurred to me that I had never had much for anything I did.

This mood of mine probably intensified the surprise I felt to find that a letter for me had been pushed under my door during the interval I had been away. It was a square blue envelope, which carried my name in a bold, woman's handwriting. There was a scent of gardenia from the page when I opened it that seemed to me needlessly strong. The note read:

Casey dear, I cannot leave you the way we left. I am so worried as to what may happen to you because I think you know my deep interest. I must see you — I must — about something which will help you very much. Something about you and me. Will you come please to the Gaiety Club tonight? At half-past nine o'clock? Ask the manager to show you to my table. I need you, Casey dear. You mustn't fail me — please. And bring your flask. The liquor is not good there. That's a darling.

Sonya.

I put the note down and lighted a cigarette. My first impression was that its contents were too tawdry and banal to be in keeping with what I had understood of Sonya's character. It was more like a streetwalker's effusion than a note which she might have written. There was no subtlety or restraint in its appeal. It was the sort of note — I paused and extinguished my cigarette — exactly the sort which might have been written to bait a trap. It was no compliment to me that she should have paid so little respect to my intelligence; or Mr. Moto, for I suspected that Mr. Moto's hand was in it. The whole composition exhibited the clumsiness of some-one trying to appeal to the psychology of another race.

It made me ashamed that I had stood up for Sonya, because the writing was an indication that Driscoll had been right; that chivalry did not count. Mr. Moto must still believe that I knew something, and Driscoll believed that Sonya knew something.

It may have been a strange occasion on which to have felt grateful, but nevertheless my sensation was one of deep gratitude, because I had been given a chance, at last, a definite chance for positive action. Slender as that chance might be, and I was under no illusions on that score, now that I had the invitation, I was in a position to make a decision of my own, instead of following, as I had until then, the drift of events. If I answered that invitation, I had the possibility of finding what lay at the bottom of this business. It was my only opportunity. If I could once reach Sonya, I would not leave her until I knew. What? I could not guess what. I could not even decide upon a course of action, but I did not have much to live for.

I had my hands on something tangible at last, something which could be played to the limit. I would show them that I was better than they thought I was. I had been in tight places before that. If it cost me my life, as it probably would, I was determined to go to the Gaiety Club, wherever it might be, and see the game out to the finish. I did not care if I was completely alone; I had been alone before.

For a little while I played with the idea of telling Driscoll, but I did not tell him. In some way, I knew that my vindication lay in doing this alone.

It was half-past two in the afternoon by then. In seven hours I would be in a place called the Gaiety Club. In eight hours I might be dead. In the meanwhile I needed rest, so I took off my coat and lay down and tried to sleep.

At about five o'clock my room telephone rang. There was a Mr. Bloom, I was told, who wished to see me and I said to send him up. I was glad to see Sam Bloom, simply from a desire to see a friendly face, but I had no wish to have Sam Bloom know or become involved in anything I proposed.

"Listen, boy," said Sam Bloom, "what happened to you today? What happened on that ship? You needn't tell me — there was something wrong, I've been looking for you everywhere. Say, I began to think — what happened? You can tell me."

"Never mind," I said.

Sam Bloom sat down heavily and scowled. "I'm a friend of yours," he told me, "and I know more about this place than you do. I know you're mixed up in something. You'd better tell me what's the matter."

But I told him that I couldn't.

"None of my business, what?" said Sam. "Is it as bad as that? You don't want any help?"

I thanked him and told him I didn't and Sam Bloom flicked a card over to me.

"I'm not butting in," he said, "but in case you want anything, here's where I'm staying. All right,

I'm not inquisitive; but is there anything you want to know? I know this town."

"Do you know a place called the Gaiety Club?" I asked.

Sam Bloom whistled. "A tough joint," he said, "in the Chinese City; a dancing place. You don't want to go there, Casey."

"Thanks," I said. "Do you know a man named Wu Lai-fu?"

Sam Bloom whistled again. "Are you mixed up with that baby? Everyone knows Wu. He wouldn't seem real anywhere else in the world. He's in secret brotherhoods. He's got a finger in politics. He's mixed up in everything. I don't believe any white man alive can make him out. He started out as a boy on a junk and then he was a houseboy in a missionary family. And then some Chinese official became interested in him. Don't you have anything to do with that baby! You don't think I'm butting in, do you?"

"No," I said. "I'm obliged. Have you got a gun you could give me?"

He reached inside his coat and unstrapped a shoulder holster. "It's a nice gun," he said. "If you use it, remember it throws a little high." He looked at me and held out his hand. "You and I have been around. You know your business, Casey. If you don't want to tell anything more, don't. If you want me later, there I am. Good luck!"

"Thanks, Sam," I said again. I was more moved by his impersonality than I could have been by any warmer interest. Sam and I had been too long in a world where anything might happen.

"Maybe it wouldn't be healthy for you if I were hanging around," he suggested.

"Same to you," I answered.

"I'm not backing down," said Sam. "Do you want company at the Gaiety Club? I'm pretty good at dancing."

"No, thanks, Sam," I said.

"Well," he said, "so long!"

"So long, Sam," I said. I think both of us were quite sure that we would not meet again.

A Chinese city even as Europeanized as Shanghai is a peculiar place at night. It is filled with sounds strange to a foreigner — of street crowds, falsetto voices, and of high stringed music that strikes a rhythm different from our own. Even above the blowing of the motor horns — and every Chinese driver seems to keep his hand on the horn unceasingly — there is the padding of feet of rickshaw runners. This background of sound confuses itself with my recollection of the Gaiety Club. I think of running slippered feet and of unfamiliar enunciation; of lights and banners before shops which display unfamiliar wares — the goods of old China mingling with Japanese and English and American novelties. I think of a China meeting the impact of the West and somehow absorbing and changing the West to conform to its ancient culture. At any rate, until the hired motor set me down in front of the Gaiety Club, everything was unfamiliar.

It was left for the Gaiety Club to demonstrate how amazingly American taste and culture have penetrated the East. The club was on the second floor of a semi-Europeanized building, and, in spite of its distance from its prototypes, it might have been a second-rate Sixth Avenue cabaret, except for the Asiatic faces of the dancers. There was the same dance floor in the center of a dimly lighted room. There were the same circles of tables about it, clustered too closely together for comfort. In the same mingled auras of perfume, liquor and cigarettes the orchestra was playing the same jazz music. A crooner, even, was rendering through a megaphone a ridiculous imitation of a negro voice. The men, nearly all of them Orientals, were in European clothes. The Chinese girls wore beautiful long gowns which fitted their figures closely and seductively. A Chinese boy took my hat, and a man, evidently the manager, a fat heavy Chinese, met me at the head of the stairs, bowing and smiling as though he were on the lookout for me.

"Miss Sonya's table," I said.

"Yes, please," he answered courteously. "Miss Sonya, oh, yes, she is waiting."

I stood a second on the threshold of the room, pulling at my tie, in order that my hand might be near the shoulder holster, for I suspected that anything could happen at any time. The music continued, waiters moved from table to table with drinks.

"This way, please," said the fat Chinese, and we walked into the vitiated air of the Gaiety Club, threading our way between the tables.

Then I saw Sonya seated by the edge of the dance floor at a small round table for two. I had never seen her looking so beautiful. Her evening dress was violet, like her eyes. Her bag lay on the table before her. She looked surprisingly young. Her figure beneath the festoons of paper flowers was that of a girl in her teens. When she saw me, she waved and smiled.

"Casey, dear," she said. "How prompt you are!"

"Always prompt for you, Sonya," I said.

"Come," she said, "come sit close beside me. That is, unless you want to dance."

The orchestra was playing "The Last Roundup", old, to be sure, to anyone from the States, but perhaps still a novelty in Shanghai. I listened to the artificial syncopation and thought how far a roundup was from there.

"I'm going to my last roundup," the Chinese singer said through his megaphone, "my last roundup" . . . and I held Sonya in my arms. There never was a more perfect dancer. Her hair was brushing my cheek. Her lips were close to my ear.

"Whose roundup?" I asked her. "I got your note. Do they mean mine?"

She laughed as though I had said something casual and amusing and then I heard her whispering in my ear.

"You fool—what brought you here? I tried to make my note show that you shouldn't come. Casey, I thought you'd understand!"

"I understood," I whispered back and held her closer. "And that's exactly why I'm here. You're going to see a lot of me tonight."

"Casey," she whispered, "they're going to kill you."

"I thought so," I whispered back. "And you're putting the finger on me, aren't you, Sonya? Well, try—but you won't get away from me."

"Casey," she answered, "I can't—I can't let them kill you."

"Then what did you get me here for?" I asked. "You sent that note, didn't you?"

"Be careful," she whispered. "They're watching us. Try to laugh—try to smile. You might—even try to kiss me, Casey."

The idea amused me. I tried and she drew her head away. I've never heard anything more genuine than her laughter.

"I'm going to my last roundup," the Chinese was shouting again, "roundup."

"Casey," she whispered, "please, I had to send that note, but I made it obvious enough. He thinks — he thinks you have it on you, Casey — that message."

"Who thinks?" I asked.

"Moto," she whispered. "Casey, I ought not to tell you this but I can't help it. Why were you dull enough to come? I shall have to help you now. Casey, we're going back to the table. Then I've been told to leave you. As soon as I do, a fight is going to start. The lights are going out. What are you going to do?"

"Find out what this is about," I answered. "It was the only way I could think of to see you again."

Now that the program was laid before me, I was not particularly alarmed, because the unknown is what is most alarming. "You'd better understand me. I thought this was set for a killing, but I came to see you. I came to find out what all this is about and you're not going to get away from me this time, Sonya."

She laughed again, that ingenuous careless laugh, and moved closer into my arms. "We haven't time to argue," she whispered. "But I'll promise you this —I'll swear that I'll be waiting for you in an automobile in the street. Don't try to leave by a door. Go out a window; don't go down the stairs. Remember, nothing has happened. Look as though you loved me, Casey."

I tried to laugh. I tried to talk about something else and then the music stopped.

"I'll see you later, Sonya," I whispered. "I give you my word for it." And we walked back to the table. "Sonya," I said, "you're beautiful." And we sat down beside the dance floor.

I believed what she had told me — that she would help me. She kept talking to me gaily. I never could remember about just what, but once she said beneath her breath:

"You'd better look around you, Casey. I'm going in a minute." She did not need to tell me.

There was a waiter standing near us who looked as heavy as a wrestler. His face was dull and clay-like and his hands were not made to handle trays of dishes. On either side of us and just behind us were three tables where only men were seated. All of them were Japanese.

"Waiter," I said, and he moved toward me, "get me a bottle of champagne." I felt better when the bottle was on the table. I raised my glass and smiled at Sonya.

"Happy landings," I said, and added softly, "I believe you'll be waiting for me. I want to see you, if I get out of this."

She rose and said, "Will you excuse me for a moment?"

And I rose also and bowed. Then I sat down again, alone at my table, the fingers of my left hand playing with the bottle, my right hand moving up and down over my necktie. I tried to look deeply interested in the dancers. The music had started up again as I sat there waiting. Seconds and minutes drag at such a time, but, after all, I did not have so long to wait.

Voices in one corner of the club were growing louder, like sounds offstage. It flashed across my mind that the plan for my elimination, as Sonya had outlined it, was not a bad one; indeed it would cause scarcely a ripple of excitement if it were handled right. It would simply appear the next day that K. C. Lee, once a well-known airman, who had fallen on hard times, had been killed in a night-club brawl. It would be a natural comprehensible epitaph to nearly everyone who knew me. I had been mixed up in enough free-for-all fights before to have some idea of looking out for myself, and this was my only hope, combined with my knowledge of what was due to happen.

The noise from the far corner of the Gaiety Club grew louder. There was a shout and a table crashed. Since I fully understood that there would be no use fighting my way toward the stairs because they would expect me there, I was trying to get the plan of the Gaiety Club and the disposition of its patrons clearly in my mind.

I was hemmed in by men on three sides, by tables. A glance over my shoulder showed me that the heavy waiter was just behind my chair, probably waiting to fall on me or to knock me over from behind. He was by far the most dangerous element in the picture. For the rest, it seemed to me they had made a tactical mistake in seating me next to the dance floor, because my way across this floor was clear to a row of tall shuttered windows just to the right of the orchestra. I gauged the distance carefully, for by that time there was no doubt that Sonya was correct. Pandemonium was breaking loose in the Gaiety Club. I gathered my feet under my chair, waiting, and then the lights went out.

I do not believe they knew I was ready, and this, combined with the quickness of my reflexes, probably saved my life. At the instant the lights went, I did three things: I kicked my own table hard in the direction of one of the tables near me, I threw the champagne bottle straight at where the faces had been at the table to my left, and hurtled backwards with all my weight, chair and all, into the Chinese waiter's stomach. I must have hurt him, because I heard him scream as we went down, but I managed to roll free of him just as we touched the floor, and I had out Sam Bloom's gun by the time I had gathered my knees beneath me. Then I fired three shots fast and bounded to one side. There is nothing worse than staying in the same place when you are shooting in the dark. Then, as I started to run, they must have guessed where I was going. I heard a voice rising above the others, shouting out some order, but I maintained my sense of direction and kept my wits about me. I pride myself that I kept my wits about me so completely that the whole affair, in spite of its tumult and darkness, remains with me in a sort of geometric exactitude. I made a dive across the dance floor, bending low, slithered against a table and plop! into someone's arms.

An arm went behind my back and a hand clamped on my throat. There was no time for amenities just then, because it was my life or the man's who held me. I presented my automatic at his middle and pulled the trigger. He dropped free of me and I plowed on through a clatter of glass and dishes, and just then the lights went up, giving me a momentary picture of the Gaiety Club which looked as though a tornado had struck it.

I was just beside one of the windows. Two men across the dance hall were swinging automatics in my direction and in another split second they would probably have got me as easily as I might have hit a pipe in a shooting gallery. There was only one thing left for me, as there had been all along — to hope that the window was flimsy and that there was a street outside not too far below. I took a shot across the dance hall. Then I dove into the window, straight through it, frame and all. I could see the dusky blackness of the street just as I lost my balance and went pitching out the window. I was very lucky in my landing in that I struck the street on all fours. Though the impact was bad enough to make me groggy, my instinct made me run for the shelter of the side of the building.

"Casey!" I heard Sonya's voice call me. "This way, Casey!" I saw a closed motor with its door open. I heard the engine running as I staggered toward it. I think Sonya must have pulled me inside, because I have not much recollection of getting there. The automobile was tearing very fast along the street. Sonya's arm was around me, her hand moved gently across my face.

"Casey," she was asking, "are you hurt? You must be hurt."

I tried to answer conscientiously, but I was in no condition to take stock of myself.

"Sonya," I said, "they didn't do that very well. They thought I'd be too easy. And now I think we're going to have a little talk. That's what I came for, Sonya."

"Casey," she was touching my right shoulder — "you're bleeding! They've shot you!"

I had felt nothing, because one feels little at such moments.

"All right," I said, "they had a damn good chance" — and Sonya seemed used to such matters.

"Quickly!" she said. "Take off your coat!" The car was still going at high speed through dim streets, but there was enough light to see that my left arm was bleeding badly. Sonya ripped back the sleeve of my shirt, which was soaked with blood.

"There," she said, and I said:

"Thanks. Tear off a piece of my shirt and tie it tight. That's a good girl, Sonya." I must have been in pretty bad condition, but she acted like a nurse in an emergency ward. The bleeding stopped when she tied my arm up tight. She leaned forward and spoke to the driver.

"Well," I said, "what next?"

"I'm stopping to buy you an overcoat and a new hat," she explained. "People mustn't see you this way, Casey." The car had stopped before a half-Chinese, half-European clothing store.

"Stay here," said Sonya. "I won't leave you, Casey."

I did not notice very much what happened for the next few minutes. Then she came back with a hat and cheap overcoat and bundled it around me.

"Where are we going now?" I asked. I trusted her absolutely then, if for no other reason than because there was nothing else to do.

"We're going to your hotel," she said. "It's nearly the only place where we can be safe, I think." Her voice caught in half a sigh and half a laugh. "I've burnt my bridges, Casey. They'll know I got you away. They'll know I warned you. You and I are outlaws, now."

"Are we?" I asked her.

"Yes," she said, and I took her hand.

"All right," I said, "as long as you're one too. Will it be possible at the hotel?"

My question made her laugh again. "You have American ideas. I don't think they'll bother much. You can say that I'm your wife. Let me wipe your face clean. And put that pistol in your pocket."

I had forgotten the pistol, but there it was, still grasped in my right hand.

CHAPTER XI

I SUPPOSE they thought at the hotel that I was drunk. I might have been, for all that I remember. Sonya steadied me like a capable nurse and locked the door. I put the automatic on the bureau and wriggled out of my overcoat and found myself staring at my image in the mirror. There was no doubt that I had been through the mill. There was a gash on my scalp that was still bleeding. My shirt had been stripped off me. A sleeve of my coat was torn and bloody. My trousers were ripped at the knees.

"Casey," Sonya said, "you look dreadfully."

"You're right," I answered, "but you don't, Sonya." My hand touched something in the side pocket of my coat. I pulled it out with my flask. "I'll feel better, maybe," I said vaguely, "if I have a drink."

"You'll feel better," Sonya said, "if you let me

wash you, Casey," and turned me gently around. She was looking at me respectfully. "There are not so many people who could have left the Gaiety Club tonight," she said. "And I know what I'm talking about."

"Yes," I said soberly. She was standing beside me, as untouched and unmoved by what had happened as though it were all a part of her life. "I'm afraid you know too much," I said, and ended with an inconsequent question:

"Are you glad they didn't get me, Sonya?"

Her answer was simple, entirely devoid of emotion.

"Do you think I'd be here, if I weren't? I never thought that I should allow sentiment mix itself with this. I shouldn't have. It may be the end, perhaps, but I don't seem to mind. I've seen members of my own family shot like dogs, but I couldn't let them kill you, Casey. It was too ugly, I think, with me a part of it. You'd better lie down, Casey. I'm going to fix your arm."

There comes a time when events are moving so fast that one's mind becomes immune to new impressions, which I suppose is the reason that everything seemed natural. I could not think it was odd that Sonya and I should be there alone. It was what I had wanted. It seemed inevitable that we must reach some final understanding. Who was she? What was she? I knew that I would find out that night.

I stood there, holding my old flask. The leather case was as battered as myself.

"If you'll excuse me," I said, "I think I'll have a drink. Perhaps you'll have one too?"

Then I saw that something about her had changed indefinably. I noticed, as I tugged at the cup on the bottom of the flask, that her glance seemed sharper, suddenly anxious.

"No," she said. "First you let me fix your arm. Casey, please put down the flask."

Her voice was sharper, like her eyes.

"Why?" I asked. There was something different between us.

"Your arm," she said, "it may be bad for you."

She was not telling the truth and I knew it.

"What's the matter with you, Sonya?" I said. "This won't hurt my arm."

I yanked off the bottom of my flask as I said it

but I did not take a drink. Instead, I stared at the bottom of the cup — at a bit of rice paper in the bottom about the size of a paper for rolling cigarettes, with writing upon it in Oriental characters. I saw Sonya's hand move toward it and I drew the cup away. I was learning what she wanted faster than I thought I would.

"No, you don't," I said. "So that's your little game! No, Sonya, you're a nice girl, but you don't get it now." I picked up the automatic from the bureau. "Drop your handbag, Sonya!" I said. "We don't want any more trouble. We're going to get the truth right now."

A part of the truth had already come over me, stunning me completely. I knew what that paper was in the bottom of my flask. I had never put it there.

"Drop your handbag, Sonya!" I said again. "You've done a good job but you haven't done it quite well enough. It looks as though I have the message now. Not that I can read it," I added, "but perhaps before we're through you'll read it for me; and Commander Driscoll can check you up. He's here in the hotel. Do you hear me? Drop that handbag, Sonya! I don't want you reaching in it for a powder puff. I'm going to call Commander Driscoll now."

"No," she said, "no! Don't do that. You mustn't!" and her handbag dropped out of her fingers to her feet.

The nervous stimulation which had buoyed me until then had not left me. I could see Sonya with part of my mind but the rest of me was back in the cabin on the *Imoto Maru*. I had to admire the astuteness of that man named Ma, who had thought of the cup on the bottom of my flask. Where would have been a better place to have left a message to a man like me than where he must have chosen before he had been discovered? Where would there have been a place where others would have been less likely to have discovered it? It was Ma's bad luck that I had never used the bottom of the flask until that moment. He had not counted on my unnatural abstemiousness. That was all.

"No," said Sonya again. "Casey, please, you mustn't. That was why they wanted to kill you. They wanted that flask, Casey. I had to ask you to bring it — Do you remember?"

I nodded to her agreeably. "And that's why you wanted to save my life, I suppose," I said. "I'm grateful to you, Sonya."

"No," she said. "It wasn't entirely that. Casey, we must think. Let me see that paper."

I put the paper back in the cup again, snapped the cup back on the bottom of my flask and put the whole in my hip pocket. Then, bending quickly, I recovered Sonya's white handbag from the floor. I found, as I expected, a small pearl-handled automatic in the middle compartment of her bag.

"You won't need that tonight," I said, "and we're going to talk about this paper; but you won't need to see it."

She did not seem surprised by my answer, not offended. "Casey," she said, "don't you think I'd better fix your arm now? It's beginning to bleed again."

"Stay where you are," I told her. "Right in that corner of the room. I'm not going to give you the chance to knock me over the head, Sonya."

She stood watching me irresolutely. "Don't you trust me, Casey? Wouldn't you, if I promised you?"

"No," I said. "I don't see why I should. Do you?"

She moved her white hands in a sort of hopeless gesture. "Casey, someone's got to help you. Someone's got to wash your head. Someone must bind your arm. I — I want to, Casey."

"You're a beautiful emotional actress," I said. "Don't act any more. Sit down!"

She began to cry, and I knew she was not acting then. "Casey," she said, "Casey, please, I swear I only want to help you."

I felt my resolve slipping, moved by that appeal. There was no doubt that I needed someone to help me.

"Very well," I said. "But mind, I'm watching you, Sonya."

As a matter of fact, she did it very well. She took me into the bathroom and stripped me to the waist. She washed out the wound with hot water — a flesh wound, I found it was, hardly more than a graze, which would probably make my arm stiff and wretchedly sore by morning, and might also give me a degree of fever; but I doubted if it would be much worse. Then she washed my head and fetched me a clean shirt from my bag.

"You feel better now?" she asked.

I felt a great deal better and I told her so. "If you'd be straight with me," I ended, "I'd like you, Sonya."

We had seated ourselves facing each other and the room was very quiet. We seemed like old friends, and perhaps we were old friends, for nearly every semblance of pretense was gone from us.

"I'll have to tell someone," she said finally. "I'm going to tell you, Casey, because I'm all alone. I'm going to tell you and beg that you may help me."

"Is that straight?" I said. "Because that's what I've been waiting for."

She answered directly. "Yes, that's straight. I swear it. You see," she sighed, "I don't suppose that my mind is as quick as some people's. I'm rather new to this, Casey. I wasn't really brought up to it. You see, Mr. Moto guessed this noon that there was something in the bottom of that flask. I was there when he guessed it."

I forgot the throbbing pain of my arm and the dull ache of my head. "But how did he guess it?" I asked. "Have the Japanese got second sight?"

Sonya smiled, and her eyes, as they met mine, were no longer hard. "Oh, no, not that, but Mr.

Moto is clever, very clever, Casey, in some ways. He has to be, in work like his. This morning I was with him as he sat thinking, and he told me what he thought. I think he rather likes me, Casey."

"Oh," I said, "does he?"

She continued, ignoring my remark: "You mustn't blame Mr. Moto. He has a very difficult time, and sometimes he seems such a little man to do everything and arrange everything. When the ship came in, he went to the Japanese Consulate and began pacing up and down a little office, trying to reconstruct what might have happened. He began with the belief that you had not seen a message or destroyed it; then he reviewed the entire search of your things. He was completely satisfied that every inch of your cabin, bags and clothing had been searched. He was sure of that because, when you left the boat, he went through everything a second time. He was sure the clothing you wore had been searched thoroughly. There was only one thing left — your flask. They had opened the top of the flask. They had seen it was full of whisky. A message inserted in a pellet might have been dropped into the whisky, but they had shaken the flask and nothing had rattled. It was only this morning that it occurred to Mr. Moto that there might be a cup fitted onto the bottom of the flask. By what you might term the process of elimination, that cup was the only place left where a message might be left. You had taken the flask with you when you jumped overboard, but he was quite certain you did not suspect the existence of a message. He had watched you carefully when your cabin was being searched. You had given no sign of interest — not the flicker of an eyelid — when they lifted up the flask. That's about all, Casey. He was right, wasn't he? You must admit that he was clever."

I could not help but admire the astuteness of Mr. Moto — an alarming astuteness — and the complete logic of what she said convinced me that she was telling the truth; but I needed more facts than that. I had reached the end of my patience, and for once in all that transaction I had something which was close to being the upper hand.

"That's good as far as it goes," I said. "Mr. Moto was a brighter man than I am. Do you know Driscoll, of our Naval Intelligence, Sonya? I had a quarrel with him this morning, but I'll go to the telephone and call him unless you'll tell me what this message is about."

Sonya leaned back in her chair, watching me almost sleepily while her hands rested limply in her lap. "Very well," she said, "I'll tell you," and then she laughed in that light way of hers, as though she could detach herself from the seriousness of the moment and be genuinely amused.

"What are you laughing at?" I asked.

"You," she said. "Excuse me, Casey. You may not understand why it strikes me as funny that anyone like you should be involved in this, and that I should be here compromised with a strange American. You are so different from what you ought to be, to appear in such a situation. You aren't devious. You're honest, Casey. You have no real awareness of the intrigue around us. Don't be angry with me. I'll tell you. I don't suppose you even remember my last name."

"Karaloff," I said.

"But it doesn't mean anything to you, does it, Casey?"

I shook my head. "Only that it's your name, Sonya."

"And the name Alexis Karaloff? Think — have you ever heard that name?"

I shook my head again and she shook hers back at me mockingly. "You never heard of Alexis Karaloff? Or of his work with crude petroleum? Or of his improvements on the Burgeius formula? Yet here you are. Even Wu Fai-fu thought you must have some idea. He told me that he asked you."

"I'm glad you think it's funny. Just who is Alexis Karaloff?" I asked.

Her expression grew set. "Your tenses are wrong. He was my father, Casey — a kind father. I heard he was dead today." She paused a moment and caught her breath. She was tragic, sitting there, but not intentionally tragic.

I said, "I'm sorry, Sonya," and put my hand over one of hers.

"Thank you," she answered. "We're used to death in Russia, Casey. I have suspected he was dead for quite a little while. But now I know, it's worse than I thought. It leaves me all alone except perhaps — "

"Perhaps what?" I asked her.

"Except perhaps for you. I'm not lying, Casey. You and I are both alone. I hope you'll understand what I tell you. You would, if you knew Russia; but you don't. I hope you'll not think it is too fantastic. You've probably heard so many Russians telling tales of greatness. The illusion of old grandeur grows on one, when one has not got it left. But this is true, Casey. The Czar was my father's patron. My father was a naval inventor. He was interested above everything else in oil as a fuel for naval vessels. He was very loyal to the Czar. I was a little girl then — too little to remember much. At the time of the Revolution he left Russia. My mother was murdered in the streets. He took me to Harbin after the Kolchak fighting. He was too much involved in the White Russian army ever to cross the border again. . . . Have you ever seen Harbin?"

"No," I said. "I had hardly heard it spoken of until I came to the Orient, Sonya."

She sighed and closed her eyes and then opened them. "Harbin," she said softly. "I wish you could have seen it when things were going well. It's my city, where I spent my childhood, Casey — a strange city of exiles; but it was gay. We Russians were always gay even when we were sad and beyond all hope. If Harbin were what it used to be, it would be the place for you and me. You should have seen the cafés and heard the singing. You should have seen the hospitality. No one thought of tomorrow in Harbin except to think of Old Russia coming back. Everyone was an aristocrat." She smiled slightly. "Whether he was or not, you understand. Harbin — the boats on the Sungari River — you should have seen the boats. You should have seen the lumber and the grain. We lived in Harbin, you see." She paused and, as her voice stopped, illusion stopped with it. I had been able to understand vaguely something of the life she was trying to tell me, when it was expressed in the soft modulation of her voice; but when she stopped, we were back in the hotel bedroom, no longer in Harbin.

"Go on," I said, "if we're getting anywhere."

"Harbin," she said; her voice was softer. "Have you ever heard it called the Paris of the Orient? It is the last city of my people, the *émigrés* from Russia. You see the rest of us scattered here in China — Russian policemen, Russian women in Chinese clothes begging on the street, Russians dressed like coolies working with the coolies on the docks —

but it was gayer in Harbin. There was quality and rank. Old generals, admirals, scholars, ladies and gentlemen from the old nobility. Why, our merchants could even compete with the Chinese storekeepers in Harbin. You should have heard us talk, Casey. There was great talk in our parlors because there was always hope, you see. Red Russia could not last. It was incredible that it could last. We were always plotting for a *coup,* building castles in the air. We were always thinking of how to seize some part of Siberia. Old officers would talk of smuggled arms and of ways to set up a Russian kingdom in Mongolia or around Bakal. We are fine people for theories, Casey. We can make them logical through self-hypnotism. You should have heard all the names that were mentioned — secret correspondence with this one and that one. I suppose it was the same in France when the old régime fell down. They would whisper about Horvath and Kolchak and Semenov. They would be buoyed up by hope. There would be talk of some mythical help from Chang Tso-lin, the old marshal, you remember, and, later, the young marshal. Chinese are like us in that way. They all of them love to talk. Then later there were dealings with 'little' Hsü, who was darting over Mongolia in his motor cars. And then there was that impresario, the Buddhist Baron Ungern Sternberg. Oh, I can give you lists of names. That was the atmosphere I was brought up in, Casey — sitting in my father's house, listening to him talking as he pored over maps and figures with strangers late at night. I have never known half of the logic of his theories. Perhaps they made no difference. Perhaps — I wonder, Casey — perhaps my father did not believe them. After all, he was a scientist who spent most of his day with his drawings in his laboratory, for he had brought some money out of Russia. I am not sure. Perhaps he did believe them. If we are unhappy, we always try to imagine something different, don't we?"

"Yes," I said, "I've imagined a lot in the last few years. Do you mind my saying this doesn't sound practical, Sonya?"

She smiled inquiringly, as though she did not understand. "Practical?" she said. "Of course, we are not practical. Have you read our literature; have you heard our music, Casey? Not much of it is practical but some of it is beautiful. We are creative artists, Casey, but my father did one thing that was practical back there in Harbin. He invented a process of treating crude petroleum, and an especial burner, which would make one gallon of oil do the work two gallons had done before. You see the implication, Casey? Japan did, when he took that invention to Japan. It meant that a warship would have twice the cruising radius that it ever had before. Can you wonder that Japan was interested? Can you wonder, Casey? My father did that — Alexis Karaloff did that. He may have been a visionary but he was a scientist. I think his name will be remembered for a long while after you and I are dead."

I tried to get my thoughts together. At last the light was dawning on me. "Do you mean that the Japanese navy is going to have a cruising radius twice as great as ours?" I said. "Why, that's going to eliminate coaling stations. It's going to change every base. If there should be a war — " I stopped.

At last I understood why Driscoll told me the matter was important. It still seemed hardly credible that such an invention should not have come from our own laboratories instead of from a city called

Harbin. If she was telling the truth, and I believed she was, any nation in the world would have struggled for such a discovery.

"Has Japan got his plans?" I asked. "Tell me what happened, Sonya?"

"I'm going to tell you, Casey," she answered. "I'm going to tell you, because it seems the only thing left to do, and because my father would have agreed with me, I think. He did not care very much about himself. Do you think many people do, who live in a world of intellect? He really cared for only two things — the abstract complications of ideas and the Russia of the old régime."

"Didn't he care for you?" I asked.

She considered a moment before she answered. "As much as he could for any human being, I think, but his opinion of the human race was not very high, Casey. Never mind about that. He appreciated the value of that invention and its significance and implications as keenly as any industrialist, without ever wishing that value for himself. He wished it to further his fixed idea. You guess the idea, perhaps? I am sorry that I have no particular knowledge of its details, but at any rate, they do not matter. It was another one of those whispering plots of my people, but this time I think it had some basis, slight as it might be. For once, they were not pinning all their faith on the dreams of some adventurer. Yes, there was a semblance of reality this time. It had to do with the concentration of Red Russian troops on the Manchurian border, when Japan became interested in the adventure of the State of Manchukuo. It seemed to my father and his friends that Japan might welcome and even might help White intervention along the border by supplying arms and money. There was one of those usual plans, perfectly logical down to the last detail. As I say, I do not know it. I only know that my father brought me with him down to Tokio and that he was greatly excited. He offered his formula and his drawings to the Japanese Government in return for their support of a White adventure, and they accepted. They had reason to accept. He was very happy until he found out that the political balance had been changed. First the Japanese hesitated to supply arms and then they entirely refused. My father felt that he had been betrayed. He left Tokio and started for Harbin, as though Japanese troops and spys were not everywhere in Manchuria. He was allowed to leave Tokio readily enough, because he had already handed over his drawings. It was some days later before they understood the plans were not complete. My father had taken the page of the chemical process back with him to Harbin and nothing was of any use without it. He was planning to sell it elsewhere, of course. He even began starting negotiations with America through the agency of the man you've seen — Wu Lai-fu. But you can guess the rest of it. This may not be the sort of life you're used to in America, but believe me, there is plenty of it here, where all life is unsettled, where there may be an explosion at any time. That is a period which develops men like Mr. Moto and Wu Lai-fu, but you can understand what happened."

"Perhaps," I said; "but you'd better tell me, Sonya."

She leaned back wearily and closed her eyes. "The Japanese were not going to let such a secret as that go, and I don't blame them much, do you? They caught my father in Harbin. They made him a political prisoner in the new capitol of Manchukuo —

high-handedly perhaps, but they had reason to be high-handed. They held him while they searched for papers in his house, but they could not find what they wanted. Then they approached me. I had received my education in Tokio, you understand, and I have many friends among the Japanese. I was approached and asked politely if I could not help in this hunt for the paper, and there was a hint that my father might not live if it were not found. I wanted him to live because I loved him, but perhaps you can imagine now why they did not find the paper. I had no intimation of it until we were together on that ship and there was a dead man in your cabin."

"Perhaps I could guess," I answered, "but you'd better tell me, Sonya."

"It was Ma," she said. "Ma was my father's old interpreter and servant, a very faithful, absolutely reliable man devoted to my father, as Chinese occasionally become devoted to their masters. I have known him ever since I was a little girl, and he would have died for us any time. As a matter of fact, he did die, didn't he? . . . What happened is clear enough now. My father, when he knew he was going to be taken, gave Ma that formula and I rather think told him to try to sell it to America. Ma escaped with it but was afraid to have such a thing on his person. He left it somewhere in Manchuria. The message, I think, was to tell us where that paper is." She paused as though she expected some response from me, but I did not answer her. "Then I heard the rest of the news today. It came from Wu Lai-fu. He has all sorts of devious connections. I think he is one of the Chinese who is secretly financing bandits in Manchuria. There is no penny-dreadful novel more lurid than parts of China and Manchuria these days. He had word, and he tells the truth, that my father was shot, trying to escape. I've been telling you the truth too, Casey. And that's about all there is. I have told you because I want you to help me. I owe nothing further to Mr. Moto. . . . Will you show me what is written on that paper in your flask?"

I paused awhile before I answered, trying to make up my mind. I paused, but I believed every word she said, however incredible it may sound as I have set it down on paper. Words in black and white about such matters as I have tried to describe do not convey any great basis of credibility, because the time and place do not go with those words or the personality which spoke them. There is no way which I know for me to convey the impression of her voice, or for me to describe the restlessness of Asia, since both of these are wholly indescribable to anyone who has not known them. I can only say again that I knew she told the truth. I knew it, if only from the way her story fitted with the small details I had seen. Her rôle was clear at last and Mr. Moto and Driscoll and even Wu Lai-fu came into place, cleverly and perfectly. More than anything else I knew that she was telling the truth because I liked her, and I have found it pays to trust quite implicitly to one's instinctive likings.

"Sonya," I said, "I think you're being straight with me."

"I am," she said. "I am." And her fingers gripped my hand. The pressure of her fingers reminded me that I had been holding her hand all the while she was speaking.

"If you see this message," I asked her, "what are you going to do?"

"I'm going to find that paper, if you'll help me, Casey."

"If you find it," I asked, "what will you do then?" She was no longer candid. She did not meet my glance.

"We'll talk about that later," she said. "The point is, we both want to find it, don't we? Will you take out your flask?"

"Yes," I said, "I'll trust you, Sonya. Can you read Chinese?"

She nodded, and I drew the flask from my hip pocket. I snapped the cup off the bottom and handed it to her.

"With my compliments," I said.

She took the cup and lifted out the paper very carefully between her thumb and finger and bent over it, first thoughtfully, then incredulously.

"Why," she exclaimed suddenly, "why — "

"What's the matter, Sonya?" I asked her.

Her eyes were fixed on mine — bewildered candid eyes. "Ma never wrote this," she said. "I know Ma's grass characters. He taught me when I was a little girl. Someone else wrote this — not Ma!"

There was a silence while I tried to think. Again

I knew that she was telling the truth, though the whole matter was becoming too complicated for me to understand.

"Are you sure?" I said.

"Yes," she answered, "I'm sure."

"But who else could have written it?"

"I don't know," she said. "Let me try to think." She sighed and frowned in her perplexity and said again, "Let me try to think."

It seemed to me that it would do no good for me to help her because I was entirely beyond my depth.

"If you don't mind," I said, "I'll take a drink while you're thinking," and I reached and took the cup away. Then I unscrewed the top of the flask. I was just about to pour a drink into the cup when my glance fell on the gold-washed bottom.

"Sonya," I said. "Look! There was another paper here. Look down at the bottom of this cup. You can see where it was lying. A corner of it's been stuck to the bottom. Look!"

She reached for the cup and drew in her breath sharply. She was bending over it, staring. Dimly, yet clearly enough to see, there was the outline of where a similar bit of paper had been lying. The presence of a little moisture had caused its edges to adhere slightly to the bottom of the cup. Someone had pulled it out hastily, a little carelessly. It was different from the paper in her hand. Her eyes were wide, her lips were set in a thin straight line.

"Casey," she asked, "did you do that?"

"No," I said, "I didn't."

"Then," her voice dropped unconsciously to a half-whisper, "take that cup and wash it very carefully. Dry it with a towel. Don't let your fingerprints stay on it. Someone has taken that message and left this one, and no one else must know."

"But who?" I asked. "I wonder who."

"We'll have to find out, Casey," Sonya said. "We'll have to try to — you and I tonight. After all, who would have done it, Casey? Not Mr. Moto. He only guessed this morning what was in there. Who else was there? You took that flask with you when you jumped into the river."

I had never tried to play the rôle of Sherlock Holmes before. "Well," I said, "let's try to think. Suppose you read me that message, Sonya."

She looked at it again. "Why, that's very queer," she said.

"What's queer?" I asked. "You'd better read the message."

"It doesn't say much," she answered, "but it's enough to understand. It says 'The house of Ma Fu' Shan at Fuyu.' That's what the message says, of course, but that isn't what is queer. Ma Fu' Shan was our man Ma's elder brother, Casey. I've seen him often enough. His house is not at Fuyu. Ma has often told me where he lives — at a farm village near the hills, a few miles outside of Chinchow. Casey, that message has been changed."

"Let's forget about that for a minute," I said, for I had a flash of intuition. "Whether it's been changed or not, I know where the thing is, Sonya. It's at Ma's brother's house. Ma left it there."

"But who changed the message?" she asked me. "Why?"

And then I had another thought. My mind had leapt dazzlingly from inconsequence to fact. In my excitement, I put my hand on her shoulder.

"Listen," I said, "have you thought of Wu Lai-fu? Listen, Sonya, he's as clever as Mr. Moto, isn't he?

Why shouldn't he want this for himself? Listen, Sonya. I think I can tell you what's happened."

She looked incredulous but I knew that I was right. I had remembered something which had happened back in that room of Wu Lai-fu's.

"I remember how his manner changed toward me when he was talking to me," I said. "He had someone look inside the cup of this flask, Sonya, as sure as I'm alive. When he was talking to me. I know he did. Can't you see? It was his idea to have that message changed. He knew that Moto would be after me. He knew that sooner or later Moto's mind would come to that flask. He wants Moto out of the way, Sonya, because he wants this for himself. He's probably sent someone off already."

Sonya looked thoughtful and then the lights were dancing in her eyes. "Casey," she said, "that's clever of you. I never thought it possible that you could think like that."

"Thanks," I said. "I didn't either — if you want to know."

Sonya moved, and I felt her shoulder tremble. "You're right," she said; "you're absolutely right. It's Mr. Wu. He's sent someone there already, probably by train this noon. It's too late for us now."

"Wait a minute," I broke in, for I had another idea. "I don't know anything about this country. How long does it take to reach this place, wherever it is, by train?"

Sonya frowned again. "Quite a time, I think. You would have to go by way of Tientsin and through Shan-hai-kwan."

"That means nothing to me," I said. "Would anyone starting this morning reach there by tomorrow noon?"

Sonya laughed. "Your ideas of rail travel in China are too American, Casey. It would take him another day, at least. But he's ahead. We can't catch up to him now."

"Can't we?" I said. "Have you forgotten what I am?"

"No," she said seriously. "I think you're splendid, Casey."

"Not that," I answered. "I'm an air pilot, Sonya. I doubt if Mr. Wu has thought of sending a man by plane."

She leaped quickly to her feet. "Casey," she whispered, "Casey, do you know where to get a plane?"

I nodded. "I know where I can try. And if you know where this village is on the map, I can set you down there tomorrow morning. How far away is it, do you think?"

"Five hundred miles," she said.

"All right," I said. "There's no use starting now. We can't make it in the dark."

Then her excitement left her. "Casey," she said, "Casey dear, there's no use talking this way. We can't do it at all. Moto's men are watching this hotel. We're cornered in here like two little rats."

"Oh, no, we're not," I said.

Now that I had thought of the plane, my mind was running smoothly. Now that there was no longer mystery, I could deal with actual facts. "If you do what I tell you, Mr. Moto will lose all further interest in us tonight. Sonya, are you listening to me? Get Mr. Moto on the telephone. Tell him to come up here. Tell him you've got the message. It was in the flask. Tell him I'm glad to give it to him. It's no affair of mine. There's the telephone. You go and tell him, Sonya."

Sonya stood an instant thinking and then she said, "Casey, I think you're very clever. I mean it.

234

You're brave, you're quick. I should be glad to go anywhere with you, Casey, anywhere on earth."

"Thanks," I answered. Her words had made my own words unsteady. She had not been acting when she said them. We were friends. "The same goes with me, Sonya."

And she walked to the telephone and lifted off the receiver.

"Remember," she said quickly, "clean out the inside of the cup, Casey dear. And you'd better show it to me when you've finished."

Not being able to understand Japanese, I have never known what Sonya said. As a matter of fact, I did not mind any longer, because I trusted her. We were like very old friends as we waited for Mr. Moto.

"You must put on a tie, Casey dear," she said, "and put the flask back in your pocket. I want you to look nice when Mr. Moto comes. Perhaps it would be just as well to put those pistols in the bureau drawer."

"You're sure we won't need them?" I said.

"Why, Casey," she looked shocked; "that isn't kind of you. Why should there be, when Mr. Moto is getting what he wants? He's not a villain, Casey. He is a very considerate man."

Her remark struck me as amusing, now that I had encountered several examples of Mr. Moto's consideration, including a bad arm and a lacerated scalp.

"No," she said, "Mr. Moto will treat you very nicely now."

I was curious to see. Sonya was picking up the room and making it presentable. From melodrama the situation seemed to turn into something almost resembling a tea party.

"Casey," Sonya said again, "since when have you had a drink?"

I tried to think back. "I have not had a drink for hours, not since at Mr. Wu's," I said. "I don't believe I need to drink, if there's anything that interests me."

"Do I interest you?" she asked.

I told her that she did and she looked pleased. The Gaiety Club and sudden death and White Russian plots of Harbin had dropped away from her.

Mr. Moto would appear with an armed bodyguard, I thought, since he would be suspicious of some trap, but I did not give his perspicacity sufficient credit. Mr. Moto came alone, without a suspicious glance. He was dressed for the evening, carefully, in what is known as a dinner coat in America, and what the French call a *smoking*, an inoffensive man bowing, smiling, and holding an opera hat. He displayed his relief and pleasure by grinning so disarmingly that I very nearly liked him. There was a row of pearls on his pleated shirt front; a handkerchief was sticking neatly from his pocket; his small feet glittered in their patent-leather pumps.

"Hello, Moto," I said.

"Hello, Lee," he answered. His smile could not have been anything but genuine. "I am so glad," Mr. Moto said, "so very, very glad, but I'm so sorry for what happened tonight. I hope you have not been hurt? If we could only have reached this conclusion before — but it was my fault, not your fault."

I stood up and shook hands with him. The situation was curious and Mr. Moto's wish to be friendly was nearly moving.

"That's all right, Moto," I said. "I only wish you'd thought of the flask sooner. I didn't, Moto."

Mr. Moto laughed and even his laughter was relieved, not the studious social laughter which one hears so often in Japan. "My dear fellow," said Mr. Moto, "I am so very glad that nothing happened to you. It would have been such a mistake. And you have been so very useful. Suppose now we have a drink. Good whisky for good Japanese and good Americans."

"Out of the flask?" I asked him.

Mr. Moto laughed gaily. "That is very good," he said. "You are a good companion, Mr. Lee."

Then Sonya interrupted. "No," she said, "Mr. Lee is not drinking."

It was the first time that I had known I was not drinking.

A shadow flitted across Mr. Moto's smiling countenance and after it a light of comprehension.

"Ah," said Mr. Moto, "so that is it. You have not been drinking? I remember now. How much more fortunate it would have been if you had been drinking," and he laughed again, so infectiously that I joined him as I handed him my flask.

"There is good whisky inside that for a good Japanese, Mr. Moto," I told him. "And there is one thing which perhaps you have not noticed. There is a cup on the bottom of the flask."

Mr. Moto was being a very good fellow. He patted my arm gently.

"You are very funny, Mr. Lee," he said. "I like men who are funny. We understand jokes in Japan. We love American jokes. Will you permit me?" He took the flask and his eyes grew narrowly intent. He pulled the cup off quickly. "Ah—" he said, and he had the bit of paper in his hand.

"Mr. Moto," I said, "I want you to understand something."

"What?" he asked.

"I want you to understand that I am very glad that you have this paper," I told him. "I want you to know that I bear you no ill will for anything that has happened—not even for your talk of a flight across the Pacific. I have had a very interesting time."

Mr. Moto's face looked genuinely troubled. "Perhaps we will talk about the Pacific flight later," he said. "But now I wish not to inconvenience you. The belongings you left aboard the ship will be sent to you at once, and in the meanwhile you have been subjected to great unpleasantness through my fault, and I am very, very sorry. I understand that you are a gentleman, Mr. Lee, and I am giving this to you, entirely with that understanding. You are

239

alone here without money. You will not mistake my motive, I ask you, please." He drew in his breath between his teeth with a sharp little hiss, pulled a wallet from his inside pocket and extracted two large notes, each for five thousand yen.

"Please," he said.

I hesitated, because I did not wish to touch his money under such circumstances. Sonya's glance stopped my refusal. "Thank you, Mr. Moto," I said. "This is too much."

"No," said Mr. Moto, "no." And he made one of his curious bobbing bows. "It is nothing for the pain you have suffered. You must not think badly of Japan. Will you take it, please?"

"Thanks," I said again.

Mr. Moto was relieved. He picked up the cup again and poured himself a drink. He raised the cup, smiling at me in a most friendly way. "Good whisky," he said, "for a good Japanese. *Banzai!* And your very good health too, Miss Sonya. You have been very, very kind. I know you have had sad news today. You will not blame me for what happened, will you, Miss Sonya? Because I am very, very sorry and I like you very much."

Sonya's gesture surprised me, but it was genuine. She put her hands on Mr. Moto's shoulders. "And I like you very much, Mr. Moto," she said.

Mr. Moto tossed off his cup of whisky with a slight tremor, since the drink was probably distasteful to him, but he tossed it off because of manners.

"Moto," I said, "I take it I may come and go as I please now? You've got what you wanted, haven't you? You won't mind my saying that you make me a trifle nervous?"

"My dear fellow!" Mr. Moto answered. "This is all over between us. If there is any help you need, call, please, at the Japanese Consulate. Mention my name, please, because I am a friend. And if you come back to Tokio, ask for me, also. I wish you to like Japan. We are a small people to have come to so much, but we are a good people, Mr. Lee."

I thanked him and I meant it.

"And we will talk about flying the Pacific later," Mr. Moto said, "but—" His glance traveled from Sonya to me, "but perhaps now I interrupt?"

"No," said Sonya, "I'm going now. I've done everything, I think."

"Yes," said Moto. "You have done very, very well. May I offer to take you where you are going?" Then he turned his attention to me again. "You have been hurt, Mr. Lee," he said. "You are wounded in the head. It is nothing much, I hope. You haven't been hurt elsewhere?"

"A flesh wound in the shoulder," I answered. "It is nothing much."

"I am so sorry," said Mr. Moto. "So very sorry. May I send a physician?"

"No, thanks," I said. "Sonya's fixed me up. Good night, Sonya."

"I'll call to see you in the morning," Sonya said, "that is, if Mr. Moto does not mind."

"Mind?" said Mr. Moto. "I am delighted. You are free, as free—what is the English expression? I am ashamed I do not know. Oh, yes, as free as the air!"

I wonder if Mr. Moto ever thought again of that phrase he used—"as free as the air."

"You will not think too hardly of us?" Mr. Moto said.

"Good night, Casey," said Sonya. "I'll call to see how you are in the morning."

"Moto," I said, "if I've killed anyone tonight, I am very, very sorry."

"Please," said Mr. Moto, "you must not bother. It was duty for our Emperor, Mr. Lee, and we are all very pleased to die for him. Good night and rest comfortably, will you, please?"

"Good night," I said, and then Mr. Moto and Sonya were gone.

I stood for a moment listening, and then I looked at my watch. A year had passed, for all I could estimate, since I had thought of time, and the shortness of the actual lapse was incredible. The hands of my watch indicated only five minutes to twelve. In less than two and a half hours I had been through events which might have filled ten years of an ordinary span. I was living fast. Sonya was right. I did not need a drink. I found the card which Sam Bloom had given me and asked for his number over the telephone. I knew what Sam Bloom had said was true, that he would stand by me for anything I wanted.

"Come up here, Sam," I said. "As soon as you can, please."

"Okay," said Sam. "I'm coming."

243

He was there in a quarter of an hour, with his hat tilted on the back of his head, asking, "What's the matter, Casey?"

"I want a two-seater plane," I said, "first thing tomorrow morning. I'm flying to a village six miles outside of Chinchow."

"Chinchow," said Sam Bloom. His intonation proved that he had the map of China on his finger tips, as any good aviator must know the country where he flies. "That's between six-fifty and seven hundred miles and the Japanese will spot you when you get across the line. They'll probably shoot at you. We'd better talk about this, Casey. Why do you want to see Chinchow? It's a walled town on a plain. I can show you plenty of 'em."

I knew that I must tell him the truth, but I did not mind, because I knew that Sam Bloom would stand by me if he could. "Sam," I said, "you're an American and I'm an American. Listen to this, Sam." As Bloom listened, I remember thinking how calmly he took it, as though he understood a part already.

"Well," was his only comment. "Why don't you tell Jim Driscoll? He's in the Intelligence."

"I've told him," I explained. "I've quarreled with Jim Driscoll; and now I'm going to do the rest of this myself. If anyone is going to get these figures, or whatever they are, I think I'm in the best position to do it. All I want is a two-seater plane, Sam. Are you going to come across or not? That's all I want to know."

Bloom moved his felt hat restlessly between his fingers. "You're asking more than you think," he said.

"Probably," I answered. "I want a plane and maps."

"You'll have to refuel," he objected, "before you get back home. How are you going to do that, Casey?"

"I don't care," I answered, "as long as I get there."

Bloom rubbed his hand along the back of his hand. "There's an observation plane up at the airport," he said, "that has been assigned to me. You can have it, Casey."

"What time?" I asked.

"Eight o'clock tomorrow morning." Bloom pulled a map from his pocket and handed it to me. "It may be that I'll lose my job, but you can have it,

Casey. I'll see you in the morning. There's the mark where you're going. I'll tell you more tomorrow. And now you'd better get some sleep. Good night!"

CHAPTER XII

EXCELLENT as his suggestion may have been, like so many of one's friends' suggestions, it was hard to follow. It took me a long time to get to sleep. I was under no illusions about the next morning. From the things Sam Bloom had left unsaid, together with the gossip to which anyone in the Orient must listen, I was certainly off on a hairbrained errand. Nevertheless, I had gained a composure which arises from a definite knowledge of a mission, combined with a certain faith in one's ability. I could get a plane from one point on the map to another, even an unknown map, as successfully as any other pilot. I knew that Sam Bloom would secure me a plane, because he said he would. What reasons he might give to his superiors were up to his own invention, not to mine, but my reputation as a flyer would probably be a help. In my time I had been given the courtesy of plenty of airports.

For a while I pored over the small-scale pocket map of China which Sam Bloom had left me. It is strange how casual one's knowledge of a country is until one is actually in it. I had never been personally cognizant before of the immense area of China. A map could speak to me more eloquently than the pages of a book, as it will to any experienced air pilot. The point which I proposed to reach, fortunately for me, lay close to the seacoast, along the line of the Mukden-Tientsin Railroad, where level land dwindles to a narrow strip between the sea and a rough mountainous country. Not so far from my proposed destination was the symbol of the Great Wall of China, winding down a mountain range to Shan-hai-kwan, the frontier town between China and the new Manchukuo State. Given the proper air conditions, the flying problem would be principally a matter of following the seacoast, then across the promontory of Shantung, then over the Po-Hai Gulf, keeping land on the left, then bearing easterly along the gulf of Liao-Tung. The political implications were what bothered me most. At the time there were Japanese forces in Shan-hai-kwan, and beyond the Great Wall there were further concentrations of Japanese troops. I was fully aware that a Chinese plane would not be well received, that it might create an incident which would involve the occupants of such a plane in very real danger, if they were taken. It was my hope to keep sufficiently high and out to sea, so that we could not be observed until the last possible moment. In the end, the whole matter would come down to the question perhaps of minutes. If we could get what we wanted quickly enough, there was a chance that we could return to the plane and take off before troops should intervene; but this was a matter which lay in the future. I believed that there would be petrol enough, if we could get back to the plane, to take us to Tientsin. If I could once arrive at the airport there — and I knew there was an airport in the line of the Peiping-Shanghai air route — my intention was to leave the plane and to go as fast as I could to the American Consulate. Aside from such rough conjectures, there was obviously nothing more that I could do about the matter. It was not even worth while to weigh my chances, but there was one thing in my favor. I was definitely convinced that Mr. Moto was off the track and that I could reach the airport without interference and perhaps without suspicion. As far as everything else went, there was nothing to do except to dismiss the matter temporarily, and this was not so difficult for me as it may sound, because the life of a flyer is made up of a series of shifting crises.

I did dismiss the matter from my mind, only to have something take its place which was of greater significance — the story which Sonya had told me. I had a smattering of engineering such as anyone may gather from a study of airplane engines. I had read about the breaking down of the atom, and understood that only a fraction of the energy of fuel was expended in either a steam or internal-combustion engine; that, in spite of all engineers could do, their contrivances for propelling us on water or in air were wretchedly inefficient. If it was true that this man Karaloff had perfected, let us say, some catalytic agent which might be added to fuel oil, it was quite easily within the realm of possibility that its efficiency as an energy-producing force might be doubled. Granting this accomplishment, even a tyro like myself could gather the immensity of its implication. On the water or in the air everyone was struggling to increase the cruising radius of vessels or of planes. Given an oil fuel of double its present power, a Japanese cruiser division could raid the Pacific Coast in the event of war and return without refueling. Nor was that all. If such a discovery should be known to all the world, it was incredible what might happen. Spheres of influence might be doubled and there would be any number of possible clashes before new spheres of influence could be established. The possibilities and complexities were too many to be grasped. There was only one thing I was sure of: with Japan the sole possessor of this secret, the influence of my country in the Pacific would be gone, and my country itself might be in danger. The idea was so apparent that I was tempted to go to the telephone and call up Driscoll, yet on second thought this seemed to me to be of no great use. If anyone could get this paper composed by this scientist who was Sonya's father, I stood as good a chance as any of my countrymen, particularly as I knew that we did not have a very closely knit Secret Service in the Orient. I may have been mistaken, but at any rate I made the decision to keep the matter to myself, and lay on my bed fully dressed.

In spite of the throbbing of my arm and the pain of my head, I went into a deep sleep and that was something I can be grateful for; if anyone needed sleep, I did that night. I was better when I was awakened in the morning at seven o'clock by the hotel porter who brought me my bags from the Japanese ship, exactly as Mr. Moto had promised. I was glad to get into my own clothes again. Although my arm and head were aching, I felt better. I put on a good heavy winter suit and a sweater. I looked over my maps also, which I had purchased for that Pacific flight—it seemed a thousand years ago—and found a larger-scale one among them of the China Coast. Then I took Sam Bloom's automatic and put it back in the shoulder holster.

At a quarter before eight the telephone rang and Sonya's voice answered to say that she was waiting downstairs. Five minutes later, just as I finished my last preparations (I had taken out a leather coat and my own goggles and helmet from my baggage),

Sam Bloom called up to say that he was waiting too. Everything was going very smoothly, but I was not surprised, for life is much like that, like a gambler's run of luck — first a number of ill chances and then everything's smooth.

Bloom was waiting at the hotel desk and Sonya was seated near him, but he did not see Sonya's connection with the business until I told her to come ahead.

"Say," said Sam, "that's the girl on the boat."

"Never mind," I told him. "Sonya's coming with me. She'll want some leather clothes. Hers don't look very warm." Sonya looked more ready for a walk along the Bund than for a seven-hundred-mile trip in a plane. There was an automobile waiting for us, and again everything went easily. Once the surprise of seeing Sonya was over, Bloom began talking to me, giving me technical directions.

"She's an observation plane," Sam said. "A Davis M type; you'll like her, Casey. Any fool can handle her. She has extra fuel tanks installed. She's good for seven hundred miles. And maybe two hundred more. I'm not asking a single question because I don't want to know what you're doing. They're glad to let you use her to try her out, because you're a well-known flyer. I don't know where you're going. It isn't my fault what may happen."

"Thanks, Sam," I said.

"You'll find maps," Sam went on, "and thermos bottles and sandwiches. Keep her up around eight thousand feet, and when you get to the gulf get twelve thousand altitude and keep as far from land as you can. Don't swing over the railroad until you have to. There are troops at every station, but I don't have to tell you about flying, Casey."

"Thanks, Sam," I said.

"That's all right," said Sam. "She's warmed up now. You can go as soon as we get there."

We were getting clear of the traffic by then. "Sam," I said, "is anybody following us?"

Bloom looked out the back window of the car. The corners of his eyes wrinkled and he shook his head.

"No," he answered, "I don't think so, and if they are, believe me you're going just the same."

There is a similarity about all airports and this one at Shanghai was no exception to the general rule. Our car drove into a dusty open space. A single-motor plane was being warmed up in front of a hangar and the motor sounded well. I was pleased to see that the ship was a model which I had flown before. She should be good for a hundred and fifty miles an hour, cruising speed, once I got her in the air. Sam Bloom was bringing out a coat and helmet for Sonya. The noise of the engine was deafening. I took Sonya by the arm and shouted in her ear.

"Are you all right?"

She smiled at me and nodded, as though we were not going anywhere.

"All right," I said, "let's go!" She climbed into the cockpit behind me and I turned around and spoke to her again. "If you want anything, write me a note," I shouted. "You think we can get what we want in twenty minutes after we land?" She nodded, smiled and patted my shoulder; then I sat down at the controls. Sam Bloom and I shook hands.

"Good luck!" he shouted. "I'll take care of things this end. Take her back into Tien-tsin."

"Tell Driscoll if I don't get back," I called back. I had turned back to the controls by then, but just as I did so, I saw a man running toward us across the field — a Chinese in a long gray gown which was flapping in the wind, and I knew who he was. He was the man who had taken me to Mr. Wu's after I had been picked up from the river. I did not care to speak to him. I gave my engine gas and pointed my ship into the wind. When we were off the ground, I circled for altitude up and up, until the tall buildings of Shanghai and the canals and rice fields of the Yangtse delta all came into a curious order, as events in a life do when one is far enough away from life. Then China was like a map such as I had seen the night before. We were circling up into a fine clear morning sky. When my altimeter read eight thousand feet, I flattened out and took my bearings; then we were going seemingly slowly, though the speed was a hundred and fifty miles an hour.

Sonya tapped my shoulder and handed me a note. "Casey," it read, "you're very nice."

There is no need to describe that flight. I have not the literary gift to convey the sensations of flying. The visibility was good and the air was clear, and there is nothing like the air at such altitudes as that. All the trappings of the world are out and one is close to the infinite in such air. The throb of the motor has always seemed to me like the drumming in one's ears when one takes ether. A flight is a sort of oblivion. I am happier in a plane than I ever am on land, I suppose because I was born for it. I am capable in the air and more alive than I am on earth. When we die, I hope our souls go to the air out of the world, up above the cloudbanks where the sun streaks down on oceans of pink and gold. There is a beauty in it which is greater than the beauty of the sea, but I am not here to write an esthetic essay. I am here to stick to facts. Sam Bloom's maps were excellent. With my mapboard and my instruments, I should have been incompetent, if I had not reached my destination, particularly given good weather. The clock on the instrument board pointed somewhere before the hour of two when I knew we were getting near.

We were swinging in toward the land over curious muddy water — water that held the silt of eroded Chinese hills and fields. We were down to five thousand feet by then and out ahead I could see the ribbon of the railroad track and the orderly outlines of a great walled town near it. Beyond, in-land, at the base of bare brown hills, there was a smaller village which appeared to be built entirely out of earth, so that it looked like something from the insect kingdom. I saw the glint of running water near it. I turned and looked at Sonya and pointed.

She nodded but I did not need any confirmation. My map told the story, and my instinct backed it up. There was the village we wanted.

I wrote another note. "We're coming down. Soldiers will see us by the railroad. We must hurry, Sonya." Then we were coming down fast, in a side-slip. The wind had tossed up clouds of dust which gave me its direction. The earth was coming up to meet us, growing clearer, clearer. We were coming down to realities again. We were coming to a land that was brown, still untouched by the softness of spring, down toward bare flat fields where men were moving like pygmies, down to that town of earth. It was a fine place for a landing. I had shut off the motor as the land was coming up. The wind was singing through the struts wildly in the most beautiful tune I know. The land was coming up with the speed of an express train. We landed well, almost without a bump. We were taxiing across a ploughed field straight toward the wall of mud surrounding low mud houses, with willow trees jutting up above their roofs, and with a rising tier of bare hills beyond them. A lonely place, a cold country that reminded me of parts of our own West. I had done what I set out to do. We had come to the town where the brother of Sonya's father's man Wu had his dwelling place.

The strange thing was how easily the matter went, although I have observed that an anticipation of difficulty sometimes makes difficulty vanish. Again, perhaps the actuality seemed simple because of my interest in everything I saw, for it was the first time I had ever seen a Chinese village with habits, architecture and customs that might easily have dated to the Stone Age. I crawled out of the cockpit and helped Sonya down to the yellowish-brown earth. We both of us were tired and stiff and deafened by the drumming of the motors and by the change of altitude. The sight of both of us appearing so suddenly from the sky had drawn the village out, gaping, large-boned men and women in coarse blue clothing that was stained from their labors.

They were the servants of the soil, the peasantry whose prototype exists in every country in the world where man gains his sustenance from the earth.

"Sonya," I asked her, and I steadied her for a moment until she was used to the solidity of the ground, "can you talk to them? We'll have to hurry, Sonya."

"Yes," she answered. She smiled at the crowd reassuringly and used her gift of tongue. Whatever she said appeared to please them, because they smiled a little stupidly, still half comprehending perhaps, and pointed to the wall. An old man moved toward me deferentially and felt timidly of my leather jacket. The children were staring at my goggles; when I pulled them up from my eyes to my forehead they gave a sigh of wonder.

"Come," said Sonya. "It's all right, Casey. Ma's brother is here in the village. We must go and find him. No, we don't have to! Here he's coming now!"

A tall Chinese in a long blue gown was walking toward us in swift easy strides. His skin was swarthy and coarsened from the weather, but I could distinguish the resemblance between him and the dead man on the boat, and plainly he and Sonya knew each other. He placed his palms together and smiled and bowed, and the red button of his skull-cap moved in an arc with the nodding of his head. After they had spoken for a moment Sonya said to me:

"Come, Casey, he will take us to his house."

We hurried, stumbling across the plowed field to a little path winding toward the gate, with half the village trotting behind us, making low polite remarks. There was a god above the gate and a little mud shrine stood just inside, with another god in the niche.

"He is the God of Learning," Sonya said. "The scholars burned prayers before him in the old days when they studied for the government examinations. Have you never seen a Chinese village?"

"No," I said.

"I'm sorry," Sonya answered, "that we haven't got more time. They are pretty places, Chinese villages, and the people need so little to be happy."

We were walking along the main street, and it was like looking at some picture I had seen before, but had never believed till then.

The combination of complete simplicity and of

a sort of airy beauty with it fitted with that interval in the sky, and the place was unrelated to anything which I had ever seen. The walls, the houses, even the roofs were made of beaten earth, but the proportion of the houses was wholly perfect. The roofs had fanciful curves, the lattices of the paper-covered windows each was different from the other, and nearly every house had its own wall enclosing a courtyard. A man was drawing water from a well beside the street, and there was a small temple near the well.

"The God of Health is there," said Sonya. "And probably the god of weather."

It was a place of strange gods, and simple suspicions hovered over it. Ma's brother walked before us and I saw that he was very worried. He obviously wanted us to get away, and I could not blame him. There would be ugly questions from the authorities about a plane which had landed.

"He tells us to be quick," said Sonya.

"That goes for me," I said. "We can't be quick enough."

The man had stopped at the gateway leading to one of those mud courtyards and was gesturing to us to enter. It was a homely place, reminiscent of a peasant's yard in northern France. Two bullocks were tethered beneath a mud-roofed shed. An old dog chained near them rose stiffly and began to bark. Some hens ran away from us, cackling. A woman was turning a stone handmill. Ma's brother walked straight across the court and opened the door of a low building and ushered us into an empty room, evidently the family living quarters. There was a stove made out of mud bricks, with a copper teakettle boiling on the top of it. The flue from the stove buried itself in a raised platform, covered untidily with bedding. There was a crude wooden dresser with utensils on it, a wooden cupboard, probably for clothing, and that was all. I had never seen such complete stark poverty or such grim efficiency. It would have been hard to have found a better place to have left that paper, for no one would have thought of looking there for anything of value.

Sonya must have understood my thoughts because she said:

"Ma's brother is a rich man, but he keeps his money hidden somewhere underground. There is probably a little hoard somewhere beneath the floor of nearly every house here. One must be careful not to look rich in unsettled times."

Sonya was talking, but her mind was not on what she was saying . . . unsettled times. Sonya had seen enough of those to be completely familiar with their developments. She was at home in that place, at home, but her mind was on something else. Her glance was strained, expectant. She was watching Ma's brother move over to that raised platform. He was lifting a corner of the matting which covered it. He was drawing out a sheet of paper about the size of ordinary foolscap. He handed it to Sonya with a bow. Her hand trembled as she took it. She bent over it attentively. Then she turned to Ma's brother and smiled. She had opened her purse. She was giving him money.

I did not have to ask her if she had found what she wanted.

Ma's brother was expostulating and his voice and Sonya's answered each other for almost a minute, in a half-comprehensible dialogue, while I stood watching. I could half imagine what they were saying, because Ma's brother pushed away the money.

He was saying he did not wish it because he was an honorable man.

Sonya's voice became more insistent. She was saying something which was important, as I could gather by the attention with which the tall Chinese countryman listened. She must have alluded to me at some point, because he turned and looked at me thoughtfully and impersonally. Then he took the money, bowed himself to the door, leaving Sonya and me standing there alone.

She had changed, now that she had the paper in her hand, displaying a new sort of gravity, a new sort of decisiveness. The paper had come between us, making us both a little different.

"So that's it?" I asked. "That's the thing you wanted?"

Sonya sighed. "Yes, Casey," she said slowly; "that's what we wanted."

I reached toward the paper, but she drew it away from me.

"No," she said, "please, Casey dear. If I could, I'd let you see it."

"What do you mean?" I asked. "Sonya, what's changed you?"

She sighed again and her voice was gentle.

"Casey dear," she said, "I want you to understand. If it were only you or me, you know I'd do anything—anything. I want you to know that. I wanted to be alone with you for a minute, and that is why I sent the man away."

I did not follow her. "What do you mean?" I asked. "We've got what we wanted, Sonya. We'd better get out of here. We'll have to leave right off."

Sonya shook her head and her lips trembled. "No," she said; "please, Casey, you don't understand. You must go, but I'm not going."

That speech jolted me into stupidity. "You're not going with me?" I said. "Why, what's the matter, Sonya? Aren't we friends?"

"Casey"—her voice was imploring—"Casey dear, I like you better than anyone I know; that's what I want you to understand. I'd do anything for you if it were only me; but in a matter like this, please, don't you see that friendship doesn't count? Casey, I want you to see. I'll tell you something else to make you understand. I think I love you, Casey. I've never loved anyone before as much as I love you, but it would make no difference, Casey. You

266

see I'm going to take this paper, because it is not mine. I know what my father would wish. He would wish me to take it to friends of his in Harbin. He would want them to use it to help what he was planning. It was a cause he was thinking of. There's something here which will help, Casey. Don't worry about me. Ma's brother will take care of me. I'm used to being alone."

Everything she said was so unexpected that I could not get my thoughts straight. Yet I should have known long ago that Sonya would have such an idea. I thought of what use she had made of me, but I could not be angry. Instead, I felt kindly toward her. Instead, I was deeply moved.

"So that's your game," I said. "I should have known it, Sonya."

"Casey," she answered, "Casey, please—"

"Sonya"—I tried to control my voice—"I don't believe you understand. I've come to get that thing you're holding, and I'm going to get it. Do you think I'm going to risk my neck and then let you take it away, so that you can sell it to someone else? Sonya, listen, please. I can understand you, but your ideas are wrong. Who are your people? What can they do? I heard you talk of them last night. You love them but you know that anything they try hasn't much validity."

"Perhaps," she said; "but that makes no difference, Casey."

"I'm sorry, Sonya," I said, "but it does to me. Think of yourself. You're alone in the world. I'd be glad to look after you. I can do it, Sonya. I don't want to talk about patriotism, but I'm going to have that paper. You and I are here alone. I'm stronger than you are. Will you give it to me, please? I don't want to take it from you, Sonya."

She appeared surprised when I had finished. "Casey," she asked me, "do you really think it is as easy as that? Do you really think — "

"Sonya," I said, "if you think I'm going to let you take this away, you're mistaken."

Sonya's voice grew calmer. "Don't think that I have not a respect for your ability," she said. "I'm sure you'll do anything you can, but you can't do much. You see, Ma's brother understands. Casey, why do you think I talked to him so long? They will stop you if I tell them to. They will come in if I call."

"Try and call," I said; "and I'll drive everyone out of this village."

"Don't," said Sonya sharply. "Please wait a minute, Casey. You mustn't! You don't see! One of the things they'll do is to smash your plane. There are men out there ready to break it if they hear a single shot — and where will you be then? Where will you go? What can you do? They'll call for the soldiers, Casey. There's no place for you to hide."

There was truth in what she said, but truth and logic did not matter to me. There are times when it does no good to weigh the pros and cons of a situation. I was convinced that this was one of those times. There was only one reason why I hesitated — because I was sorry. I knew that I would not see Sonya again.

"Sonya," I said, "I'm sorry."

"So am I," she answered. "If you're going now, I'll go to see you off, but you mustn't wait any longer."

"Sonya," I said, "it seems to me you're fixing it so that we both have to give up everything for nothing. I don't want you to think I'm not fond of you, because I am. I don't like to think how different things might be."

"Please," she said, "please don't say that."

"All right," I answered. "Have it your own way, Sonya."

She must have been taken off her guard. If she was, it was exactly what I intended, much as I hated what I was prepared to do. She may have forgotten momentarily that she was still holding that sheet of paper.

I half turned, reluctantly, as though I were going to go. Her hand and the paper were out of my line of vision for a moment but I knew exactly where it was. I darted sideways. My fingers reached the corner of the paper and I snatched. If I had thought I could be too quick for her, if I had thought that I could snatch the paper out of her hand, I was mistaken. Her hand drew back the instant mine caught the corner of the page. There was a tearing sound and Sonya had stepped away from me. We each were holding a half of that foolscap and staring at each other stupidly. I think she was going to cry out but I stopped her. If I did not have the whole paper, at least I had a half.

"Be careful, Sonya," I said. "There's one thing I can do now — I can destroy this if you call."

She understood me. At any rate, she did not cry out and I looked at my half of the torn page. There were words on it in fine penmanship in a language I did not understand, and formulas of what I knew to be organic chemistry from the groups of symbols that were bound together in valances.

Sonya was speaking gently. "That wasn't fair of you," she said.

"My dear," I answered, "do you think you've been entirely fair? Are you going to give me that other half?"

"No," she said, "not as long as I live. And you won't get it, Casey."

We stood there facing each other. That short interval of time is the oddest which I have ever experienced. The surroundings made it stranger — that wretched mud hovel, the kettle steaming on the small brick stove, the tamped earthen floor, the faint light through the paper windows. I shall never live through a moment like that again, or, if I do, it will be no more credible to me than the scene through which I lived. I do not believe I exaggerate as I think of the importance attached to this paper which we sought. It may be that I am mistaken, but in my heart I am close to being sure that I held half the future of the Pacific basin in my hand as I stood in that Manchurian farmhouse, and that the girl opposite me was holding the other half. I had never realized the complete seriousness of my position until I held that paper. It was a responsibility about which I could not be entirely certain, but it was one which I had to take. My mind seemed to go in a circle, futilely seeking for another step, when Sonya interrupted me.

She was calling out for help.

I realize now that Sonya's call lifted all decision from my hands. I shifted my paper from my right hand to my left and got out my automatic just as the door burst open.

"Wait," I said. "Sonya, tell those fools to wait a minute!"

I knew already that there was only one thing left for me to do. I was even relieved by the thought and I still believe that I did what was best, and all that was possible.

Ma's brother, with a group of men behind him

(all of them big Chinese) stood irresolutely in the doorway. Some of them were holding hoes and mattocks. One of them held an antiquated rifle.

"Tell them to wait a minute, Sonya," I said.

Sonya called to them sharply. I had to make my next move quickly and accurately, before anyone could guess what I intended. There was a glow of embers in the draft in the mud-brick stove. I bent quickly, still watching Ma's brother and the men.

"Casey!" Sonya cried. "You can't do that!"

I thrust the paper into the embers of the stove while the echo of her voice still rang. A bit of flame licked up at it. The paper was on fire and I straightened up, holding the burning half sheet.

"I think that's the only answer, Sonya," I said. "I think we both did our best." The flames burnt my fingers and I dropped the charred fragments on the floor. Then I moved toward her, and I was glad, now that it was over. "I guess that's the end, Sonya. You'd better burn up your half of that. It won't do you any good, I think, but it might be dangerous. Burn it up, Sonya. I'm going to take you home."

She swayed toward me, and then she was sobbing

on my shoulder. "You're not angry," she was sobbing, "are you, Casey?"

"Yes," I said, "don't you see, everything's all even, Sonya." And a sound made her straighten.

We both knew what the sound meant. It came from the sky, reverberating between the roofs and the smoky rafters above our heads—a droning sound which grew louder, louder and then stopped. It was another plane. Its pilot was cutting off the engine, landing. Voices outside were rising in a torrent of sound.

"That will probably be the Japanese police," I said. "Give me that paper, Sonya." And I put it in the fire. "I'm sorry," I said to Sonya again and I took her hand.

"Don't be sorry," she answered. She looked happier, younger, the way she should always have looked. Her lips curled up into a smile. "Don't be sorry," she said, "because I think the police will be" —and she mimicked the English of Japanese— "very, very sorry."

"And on the whole, I'm pleased," I said; "very, very pleased. What do you think they'll do to us? Shoot us or put us into jail?"

There were no sounds from the street any longer. The villagers must have gone away and we found ourselves a minute later, staring at an old friend of ours. Mr. Moto, out of breath, was standing in the door of Ma's brother's house. Mr. Moto's composure was ruffled from his haste and he no longer wore his morning coat. Instead, his clothing was more incongruous — a tweed golf suit and a brown tweed cap. I knew enough not to laugh because Mr. Moto was serious.

"So you have not gone," he said. "You are clever, Mr. Lee. As long as you have not gone, I am very, very pleased."

"I like it here," I answered. "Why should I go away?"

"Do not joke, please," Mr. Moto said. "You cannot get away from here. We have you, Mr. Lee. And you too, Miss Sonya, and we want what you have come to find — right away, please. Do not joke!"

"The fuel-oil formula?" I said.

"Yes, please," said Mr. Moto. "Thank you so much. I am so glad you know what I mean. This is serious. I must have it, please."

"No, Mr. Moto," I answered, "I'm afraid you can't."

"Please," said Mr. Moto, "do not be funny, Mr. Lee."

I found myself close to laughter again, but I did not laugh. It would have been discourteous to laugh, when Mr. Moto was laboring under such excitement.

"The trouble was," I said, "you have wanted this and I have wanted it, and so has Sonya here. When people like the three of us want something, what happens, Mr. Moto?"

"I am being very patient, Mr. Lee," Mr. Moto said.

"The trouble was this," I explained to him. "Miss Sonya had that paper. I snatched for it and it tore in two. There seemed to be only one thing to do with that difference of opinion." I pointed to the fire. "I burned my half. Then the thing was useless. Then Miss Sonya burned her half. You can see the charred fragments on the floor. There is the story, Mr. Moto, and I am very much afraid that Japanese and American battleships will continue to burn oil in the same old wasteful way. And perhaps it's just as well. What do you think, Mr. Moto? I ask you because you're a sensible man."

I thought he would be angry, but he was not. He grew grave, as he stared at the charred fragments on the beaten earth floor. Then he looked up at me.

"Sometimes," said Mr. Moto, "I do not think, in spite of my study and my admiration for your people, that I understand them very well. But please, Mr. Lee, you are a man of honor, I think. We have tricked each other and I am very, very sorry. I do not wish to cause you further pain. Will you give me your word of honor that a single large page of paper containing chemical symbols was what you have burned?"

"I swear it, Mr. Moto," I said. "You can throw me into jail, you can strangle me, but there isn't anything left — anything at all."

Mr. Moto's forehead wrinkled. "But why should I strangle you, please," he said, "when it would do no possible good? When this is burned, we cannot help it, can we? This must conclude the matter. As long as I am sure, and I *am* sure. A little while ago I should have been relieved to know that this was

277

not in existence. . . . Yes, perhaps you are right. You have not got it and I have not got it; our nations have not got it. In one way I am very very sorry; at the same time I think I am very, very pleased. We can be friends now, I think. There is nothing more to fight about, I believe."

He had swallowed his disappointment. He no longer seemed a comical figure in his tweed suit.

"Moto," I said, "if I have tricked you in any way, forgive me. I am sure Miss Sonya means the same."

Mr. Moto removed his cap and bowed. "I have always liked Miss Sonya," he said. "Miss Sonya is very nice."

"I think so too," I answered. "I am going to marry Miss Sonya."

"Please," said Mr. Moto, "would you object if I should shake hands with her and offer her my congratulations?"

Sonya began to laugh. "Excuse me," she said, as Mr. Moto looked hurt and puzzled, "I'm not laughing at you, Mr. Moto. I'm laughing at all three of us — that we should be in a place like this."

"Oh, yes," said Mr. Moto. "Ha-ha, that is funny. Life is so very strange."

"Moto," I asked him, "would you mind telling me something? How did you get here so soon?"

Mr. Moto was still smiling. "My dear fellow," he said, "it was difficult. I understand that you know Mr. Wu Lai-fu. He saw you leaving in the plane. He had not thought of that, so of course he came to me in order to save something for himself. He told me where you were going, for a price, and I came very quickly. Mr. Wu is a clever man."

"Yes," I said. "Mr. Wu is clever."

"But then," said Mr. Moto, "perhaps we are all — you and Miss Sonya and me."

Sonya laughed again. "Too clever to be comfortable," she said. "What are you going to do with us now?"

"We will go to the military barracks," said Mr. Moto, "if you please."

"Oh," I said, "we're prisoners, are we, Moto?"

"Please," said Mr. Moto, "you must not say that. We go to the barracks to be warm and comfortable. The officers, they are good fellows, and I shall get you fuel for your plane. There is no sense in prisons. And Mr. Lee, we shall have some whisky, perhaps."

"No," said Sonya, "Casey isn't drinking."

"Oh," said Mr. Moto, "I am very, very sorry."

"So am I, Moto," I told him, "very sorry and sur-prised."

I believe I have reached the end of what I set out to write, unless Commander Driscoll has some further suggestion. Now that I have reached the end, it comes over me suddenly; it seems as difficult as the beginning. After all, exactly what did I do, I wonder? Jim Driscoll was the one who helped me out with this question. Naturally I saw Driscoll when I came back to Shanghai, and I brought Sonya with me.

"What you don't know won't hurt you," Driscoll said. "The Orient is different from America. I shall want you to lunch with the Admiral tomorrow, and then you will probably have to write this out, because it is important. There's no need for you ever to know how important. When you write it, you can say anything about me you like, but I should like to have you make one addition. I might have treated you better, Casey. We were both of us excited that other day, and let's forget it. And there's another thing — you might go and call on Wu Lai-fu. I think he'd like to see you."

So this is as far as I am going to go and further, perhaps, than I had anticipated. I have finished a narrative which is difficult to believe, now that I am away from the place where it occurred and may never see that place again.

"Don't worry," Driscoll said, "anyone who has been out here can understand that anything can happen. You ought to be grateful to the Orient."

Perhaps I am — at any rate when I think of Sonya.